Arthur D. Hosterman

Noble and Heroic Deeds of Men and Women

Arthur D. Hosterman

Noble and Heroic Deeds of Men and Women

ISBN/EAN: 9783337194383

Printed in Europe, USA, Canada, Australia, Japan

Cover: Foto ©Andreas Hilbeck / pixelio.de

More available books at **www.hansebooks.com**

MEN AND WOMEN.

ILLUSTRATED

WITH NUMEROUS ENGRAVINGS, AND INTERSPERSED WITH ANECDOTES,
INCIDENTS, AND SKETCHES FROM THE LIVES OF THE GREAT
AND GOOD, ILLUSTRATIVE OF NOBLE AND HEROIC
TRAITS OF CHARACTER.

EDITED AND COMPILED BY

A. D. HOSTERMAN.

PUBLISHED BY
FARM AND FIRESIDE,
SPRINGFIELD, OHIO.
1881.

MAJOR McCULLOCH'S DARING LEAP.—*Page* 76.

CONTENTS.

PREFACE.

There can be no doubt but that Biography and History have been of incalculable value to the world. Causes and their sequences, plans and their consummations, are followed; and man is able to learn by precept rather than by the tedious routine of experience. But in nothing more than in the impetus given to follow worthy traits of character, to study beautiful examples of pure lives, and to imitate that which we admire, is Biography and History valuable. Youth follows the experience of age, and as the example set up for imitation is good or bad, will a new generation be. A prominent educator once said that if he had the children of any country from the time of their birth until they were seven years of age, after that any school of doctrines, any influences, might be thrown around them, and he could predict what they would become in morals when men. There is much of truth in this. Early influences and impressions are always lasting. The necessity, then, becomes imperative that we place before the youth of the land models of character, both noble and brave, if the best results are to be obtained. To furnish such a coterie of incidents illustrative of noble and heroic traits of character, in which the youth as well as the aged might be interested, and hoping in this manner to be the means of doing much good, the publishers have been led to make such a compilation as the present volume.

> "And by their light
> Shall every valiant youth with ardor move
> To do brave acts."   —*Shakspeare.*

Agisilaus, King of Sparta, being asked, "What ought children to learn?" replied, "That which they ought to practice when they become men." No sentiment was ever expressed more conformable to the principles of our government. Next to their duty toward God, there is not a parent who ought not to impress upon the minds of his children the devotion which is due their country; and how can this be more effectually done than from the dawn of reason to keep in their view those virtues which have raised the benefactors of the republic to immortality?

"What is life?" has always been a perplexing inquiry. Every class of persons, if not indeed every person, has a different—either a higher or a lower—view and standard. There is one thing certain, that the brave and noble are always remembered longer and better after death; and few can deny but that this is one chief aim of life. Every man that is truly great, in whatever sphere of life he may act, has certain noble traits of character in the composition of his being. And—

> "Still to employ
> The mind's brave ardor in heroic aims,
> Such as may raise us o'er the groveling herd
> And make us shine forever—THAT IS LIFE."

The world is full of negative characters. The demand for men of thought and men of action—pure thought and brave action—constantly increases. The best illustrations of noble traits of character and heroic deeds have generally been during times of national peril, when the common pulse of a whole people has throbbed and beat quickly—when action was needed.

In our own country the Revolution and the Rebellion were the causes and the impetus to action. Not only men but women also responded. Willing to give up home, friends and family, to offer their energies and life blood, and the kindly ministerings of the women, command at once our respect and admiration. And yet we need not always look to such thrilling times for our illustrations of noble traits of character. The widow with her mite, and the self-sacrificing, disinterested actions of those all about us, bespeak noble traits and examples worthy of imitation.

We can best learn to hate cowardice and a groveling spirit by studying their opposites. Bravery and nobility of character have been honored and respected as long as man has existed. They are the cardinal virtues of true manhood or womanhood, and always command respect. It is a sacred duty of every person to make his life as grand and noble as possible; and there can be no better, no surer manner of bringing this about than by instilling into the minds of the youth such examples as are grand and noble. To build a fine, abiding and beautiful architectural structure, in which proportion and grace are blended, the first thing that is done is to build well a good sub-structure, a foundation on which to rest. Just so in forming a beautiful character. The first thing necessary is to have a pure mind, before which, as an entrancing mirror, are reflected the images and casts of noble deeds, heroic actions, and that nobility of character which is universally respected. The province of this volume is then seen. We are not pretentious enough to claim originality in the majority of the facts and incidents found in these pages. We have only aimed at an acceptable compilation, such as is found in no other work, and which the author and publishers believe will meet a demand long felt. We have had recourse to a large number of standard and antiquated works, from which we have drawn liberally. Many of the stories have been entirely rewritten and modernized. If it shall be the means of inspiring any youth to better and renewed exertions, or to spur any one to better efforts, the aim of the compilers will have been amply met. To do good has been the motive in presenting this to the public, and should it fail in this it will fail utterly. The actions and deeds herein recorded are worthy of study and imitation by all. An ambition to be noble is laudable. "By a knowledge of the lives of the great, we can regulate our own course and steer star-guided over life's trackless ocean."

A. D. H.

SPRINGFIELD, OHIO, December 1, 1881.

NOBLE AND HEROIC DEEDS

OF

MEN AND WOMEN.

GEORGE WASHINGTON.

Of this great man it was said that, "He was first in war, first in peace, first in the hearts of his countrymen;" and time has not taken any of renown from his bright escutcheon or galaxy of talents. George's father died when he was quite young, and the guidance of the future leader through the dangers of childhood devolved upon his mother. She was fitted for the high trust of raising up a deliverer for our country, and during his eventful life Washington regarded the early trainings of his mother with the deepest gratitude. He received a good common school education, and upon that, a naturally thoughtful and right conditioned mind, laid the foundation of future greatness. His culture was altogether his own work, and he was, in the strictest sense, a self-made man. Yet from his early life he never seemed uneducated. Truth and justice were the cardinal virtues of his character. Young Washington was playing in the field one day with another boy, when he leaped upon an untamed colt belonging to his mother. The frightened animal used such great exertions to get rid of his rider that he burst a blood vessel and died. George went immediately to his mother and gave her a truthful relation of all that had happened. This is a noble example for all boys. He was beloved by all his young companions, and was always chosen their leader in military plays. His mother's persuasions, at the age of fourteen, were sufficient to turn him from a wish to enter the navy. Several years of his boyhood were spent in surveying in Virginia. In the forest rambles incident to his profession he learned much of the topography of the country, habits of the Indians, and life in camp. Nature, too, revealed to him her obedience to serene and silent laws. These were stern and useful lessons of great value in his future life. Young Washington was appointed one of the adjutant-generals of his state at the age of nineteen, but soon resigned his commission to accompany an invalid half-brother to the West Indies. At the age of twenty-seven years Washington married the beautiful Martha Custis, and they took up their abode at Mount Vernon, on the banks of the Potomac. Residing there until 1774, he was chosen to fill a seat in the Virginia Legislature. The storm of the great revolution was then gathering, and toward the close of summer he was elected a delegate to the first continental congress, which assembled at Philadelphia in September. By the unanimous voice of his compatriots he was chosen commander-in-chief of the army of freemen which had gathered spontaneously around Boston. It was a fortunate circumstance attending his election that it was accompanied with no competition and followed by no envy. Washington at once moved to Cambridge, Massachusetts, and on the third day of July, 1775, attended by a suitable escort, proceeded from his headquarters to a great elm tree—one of the most majestic natives of the forest. Under the shadows of that wide spread tree, Washington moving forward a few paces, drew his sword as commander-in-chief of the American army, declaring that it should never be sheathed until the liberties of his country were established. After various vicissitudes, numerous battles, successes and reverses, of which every American is familiar, he forced Lord Cornwallis to surrender at Yorktown, by which great achievement he put an end to the active operations of the revolutionary struggle, and secured peace and independence to his country. And when the blessed morning of peace dawned at Yorktown, and the last hoof of the oppressor had left our shores, Washington was hailed as the deliverer of his people, and he was regarded by the aspirants for freedom in the eastern hemisphere as the brilliant day-star of promise to future generations. Frederick the Great declared, with reference to some of Washington's achievements, that they were not excelled in brilliancy by any recorded in the annals of military action. There is no doubt that had Washington so desired, he could have founded a monarchy, sustained by the bayonets of his army. The officers around Newburgh called a secret meeting, and finally determined upon the title of king for the head of the government. Washington spurned the gilded bribe of a king's crown, and promptly and sternly rebuked the abettors of the scheme. When the federal constitution was framed, and a president of the United States was to be chosen, according to its provisions, his countrymen, with unanimous voice, called him to the highest place of honor in the gift of a free people. Washington presided over the affairs of the new republic for eight years, and those the most eventful in its history. To guide the ship of state through the rocks and quicksands of all the difficulties that arose required great executive skill and wisdom. Washington possessed both, and he retired from the theater of public life without the least stain of reproach upon his judgment or his intentions. On September 15, 1796, Washington published his farewell address to the country he had formed—almost out of chaos. John Adams succeeded him in office, although he could have been elected a third time had not private affairs demanded his attention, and the father of his country retired to his home at Mount Vernon, followed by the love and admiration of a people who now fully recognized his public spirit, his staunch integrity, and the extent of his intellectual resources. There he died on December 14, 1799, his epitaph a nation's praise. Europe paid tribute to the memory of Washington. His name was perpetuated in the names of a multitude of American localities, and his countenance became a perpetual heirloom among his people. Napoleon Bonaparte said of this great man : "Posterity will talk of Washington with reverence as the founder of a great empire, when my name shall be lost in the vortex of revolution." Courage was so natural to him that it was hardly spoken of to his praise; no one ever, at any moment of his life, discovered in him the least shrinking in danger, and he had a hardihood of daring which escaped notice, because it was so enveloped by superior calmness and wisdom. His hand was liberal; giving quietly and without observation, as though he was ashamed of nothing but being discovered in doing good. Integrity was so completely the law of his nature, that a planet would sooner have shot from the sphere than he have departed from his uprightness, which was so constant that it often seemed to be almost impersonal. He loved fame, the approval of coming generations, the good will of his fellowmen of his own time, and he desired to make his conduct coincide with their wishes; but not fear of censure, not the prospect of applause, could tempt him to swerve from rectitude, and the praise which he coveted was the sympathy of that moral sentiment which exists in every human breast, and goes forth only to the welcome of virtue. This is he who was raised up to be not the head of a party, but the father of his country. And such was the life and beautiful example which Columbia's most beloved son left for us as a legacy.

JOHN ELIOT.

Justly termed "the apostle to the Indians," John Eliot was the most successful in his efforts to Christianize portions of the aboriginals of this country. Born in Essex County, England, in 1604, and during the decade from 1630 to 1640, he was associated with Mr. Wilde at the head of a congregration at Roxbury. Looking upon the dusky tribes around him, the heart of Mr. Eliot was troubled by a view of their spiritual destitution, and he resolved to preach the gospel among these heathen neighbors. First mastering the twenty different dialects spoken by as many tribes, he began his labors. Although violently opposed by the Indian priests, whose "craft was in danger," and also by some of the sachems and chiefs, he was not dismayed, but penetrated the deep wilderness in all directions, relying solely upon his God for protection. Finally an Indian town was built at Natick, and a house of worship—the first for the use of Indians ever erected by Protestants in America—was reared there in 1660. Still extending his labors of love, his influence became unbounded over them; and he was also their protector when, during King Philip's war, the Massachusetts people wished to exterminate the Indians without discrimination. It was estimated that there were five thousand "praying Indians"—as the converts were called—among the New England tribes when Philip raised the hatchet. When the weight of four score years bowed the pious apostle, and he could no longer visit the Indian churches, he persuaded a number of families to send their negro servants to him to be instructed in gospel truth. With the triumphant words, "Welcome Joy," upon his lips, the venerable and faithful servant died on the 20th of May, 1690, at the age of eighty-six years.

JOHN WINTHROP.

As governor of the puritan colony which John Endicott had founded at Salem, John Winthrop founded the future metropolis of Boston, because there pure water flowed from the hills. The first subject brought under consideration in his new government was a suitable provision for the support of the gospel. Mr. Winthrop was a man of great benevolence. It was his practice to send his servants among the people at meal time on trifling errands, with instructions to report the condition of their tables. When informed of any who appeared to want, he always sent a supply from his own abundance. He was also merciful as a magistrate, for he considered it expedient to temper the severity of law with more lenity in an infant colony than in a settled state. Because of his lenity toward offenders he was charged, in 1636, of dealing "too remissly in point of justice." Governor Winthrop came to America a wealthy man, but died quite poor. His benevolent heart kept his hand continually open, and he dispensed comforts to the needy without stint. He regarded all men as equally dear in the eyes of their Maker, yet his early education blinded him to the dignity of true democracy. When the people of Connecticut asked his advice concerning the organization of a government, he replied, "The best part of a community is always the least, and of that least part the wiser are still less." Worn out with toils and afflictions, this faithful and upright magistrate entered upon his final rest on the 26th of March, 1649, at the age of sixty-one years.

———

ANNE LETITIA BARBAULD.

The woman whose name heads this article was long admired for her genius and virtue. She was born at the village of Kibworth Harcourt, in Leicestershire, on June 20th, 1743, the eldest child and only daughter of John Aiken, D. D., a dissenting clergyman, who kept an academy. Her private education, the religious influences of her home and secluded life in the country, were well fitted to develop early her natural taste for poetry. Her education was principally conducted by her excellent mother, a lady whose manners were polished by early introduction into good company. In the middle of the last century a strong prejudice still existed against imparting to females any tincture of classical learning. For a long time this was denied Miss Aiken, but at length she overcame the scruples of her father and with his assistance she became acquainted with many old Latin and Greek authors. Her recollections of childhood and early youth were not associated with much of the pleasure and gayety usually attendant upon that period of life; but it must be regarded as a circumstance favorable, rather than otherwise, to the unfolding of her genius, to have been thus left to find her own objects of interest and persuit. The spirit of devotion early inculcated upon her as a duty, opened to her by degrees an inexhaustible source of tender and sublime delight, and while yet a child, she was surprised to find herself a poet. She was possessed of great beauty, distinct traces of which she retained to the latest period of life. Her person was slender, her complexion exquisitely fair, with the bloom of perfect health; her features were regular and elegant, and her dark blue eyes beamed with the light of wit and fancy. About the close of the year 1771, her brother persuaded her, and by his assistance her poems were selected, revised and arranged for publication; and when all these preparations were completed, finding that she still hesitated and lingered, like the parent bird who pushes off her young to its first flight, he procured the paper, and set the press to work on his own authority. A number of editions were gone through with; compliments and congratulations poured in from all quarters, and even the periodical critics greeted her muse with unmixed applause. In 1774, Miss Aiken was married to the Rev. Rochemont Barbauld, a descendant of French protestants. Subsequently, Mr. Barbauld opened a boarding school in the village of Palgrove, in Suffolk. This school was largely attended, and was taught in English composition by Mrs. Barbauld several times a week; the boys were called in separate classes, in her apartments; she read a fable, a short story, or a moral essay to them, aloud, an I then sent them back into the school room to write it out in their own words. Each exercise was overlooked by her; the faults of grammar were obliterated, the vulgarities chastised, the idle epithets canceled, and a distinct reason always assigned for every correction. In all the branches which she taught she attempted to relieve the dryness of the study by so many strokes of description, and such luminous views, that they were always remembered. In 1790, the rejection of a bill for the repeal of the Corporation and Test Acts, called forth her eloquent and indignant address to the opposers of this repeal. Her poetical epistle to Mr. Wilberforce, on the rejection of the bill for abolishing the slave trade, was written in 1791. To claim for this distinguished woman the praise of purity and elevation of mind may well appear superfluous. She was acquainted with almost all the female writers of her time, and there was not one of the number whom she failed frequently to mention in terms of admiration, esteem, and affection, whether in conversation, in letters to friends, or in print. To humbler aspirants in the career of letters, who often applied to her for advice or assistance, she was invariably courteous, and in many instances essentially serviceable. The sight of youth and beauty was peculiarly gratifying to her fancy and her feelings, and children and young persons, especially females, were accordingly large sharers in her benevolence. In the conjugal relations, her conduct was guided by the highest principles of love and duty. As a sister, the uninterrupted flow of her affection, manifested by numberless tokens of love, not alone to her brother but to every member of the family, were ever recalled by them with emotions of tenderness, respect and gratitude. She passed through life without having dropped, it is believed, a single friendship, and without having drawn upon herself a single enmity which could properly be called personal. The cause of rational education is more indebted to her than to any individual of modern times, inasmuch as she was the leader in that reformation which has resulted in substituting the use of truth and reason for folly and fiction in books for the nursery. She has also shown that a talent for writing for youth is not incompatible with powers of the highest order. All her compositions are characterized by simplicity of feeling, an easy flowing style, and pure and elevated sentiment.

WILLIAM PENN.

"Thou 'lt find," said the Quaker, "in me and mine,
But friends and brothers to thee and th uc;
Who abuse no power and admit no line,
'Twixt the red man and the white."

This was the guiding principle of William Penn, the founder of Pennsylvania.
Having in early life dissented from the church of his family and joined the
Quakers, he did work of proselyting, and suffered revilings and imprisonments
"for conscience sake." In 1681, wishing to establish a home for the oppressed
Friends in England, he secured from Charles II. the grant of a large tract west of
the Delaware, in lieu of sixteen thousand pounds due his father by the crown,
on condition of paying annually two beaver skins. This territory Penn wished
to have called Sylvania (*sylva*, forest) as it was covered with woods; but the king
ordered it to be styled Pennsylvania, and although Penn offered the secretary
twenty guineas to erase the prefix, his request was denied. Penn immediately
sent a body of emigrants to begin the "holy experiment," and came himself
the next year. He was royally received, for his first proclamation had preceded
him with the spirit of a benediction. "I hope you will not be troubled at your
change and the king's choice," he wrote, "for you are now fixed, at the mercy
of no governor that comes to make his fortune great. You shall be governed
by laws of your own making, and live a free, and if you will, a sober and in-

dustrious people." He founded Philadelphia—City of Brotherly Love—toward the close of the same year; and within twenty-four months afterward two thousand settlers were planting their homes there. A legislature appointed by the people was to make all the laws. Every sect was to be tolerated. Any free man could vote and hold office who believed in God and kept the Lord's day. No tax could be levied except by law. Every child was to be taught a useful trade. It seemed to be Penn's only desire to make the little colony as happy and free as could be. Penn's treaty with the Indians, "was the only one never sworn to, and the only one never broken." Penn returned to England in 1684, and through his influence with the king, obtained the release of thirteen hundred Quakers then in prison. He was himself thrown into prison upon being suspected of adhering to the fallen monarch. In 1699 he again visited America. He died at the age of seventy-four years, greatly beloved by the Indians; and it is worthy of remark that not a drop of Quaker blood was ever shed by the savages.

JOHN LAURENS.

Among the most distinguished worthies of the revolution, Lieutenant-Colonel John Laurens was one; for no man more highly merited the gratitude of his country. His general character is well known. His extensive information and classical knowledge obtained the respect of the learned. His polite and easy behavior insured distinction in every polished society. The warmth of his heart gained the affection of his friends, his sincerity their confidence and esteem. His patriotic integrity commanded the veneration of his countrymen—his intrepidity their unlimited applause. An insult to his friend he regarded as a wound to his own honor. Such an occurrence led him to engage in a personal contest with General Charles Lee, who had spoken disrespectfully of General Washington. The veteran, who was wounded on the occasion, being asked how Laurens had conducted himself, replied, "I could have hugged the noble boy, he pleased me so." His gallantry in action was highly characteristic of his love of fame. The post of danger was his favorite station. Some, indeed, may style his intrepidity, at every risk, the height of rashness. Strictly speaking, it was so. But, at the beginning of the war, when the British officers were persuaded, or affected to believe that every American was a coward, such total disregard of personal safety on the part of Laurens, such display of chivalric intrepidity, that equally excited their surprise and admiration, was essentially beneficial to our cause.

But there is one service rendered to his country, which, though little known, entitles him to its warmest gratitude. When sent by Congress to negotiate a loan from the French Government, although his reception was favorable and encouragement given that his request would be granted, yet the delays perpetually contrived by the Minister, the Count de Vergennes, afforded little prospect of immediate success. Convinced that procrastination would give a death blow to independence, he resolved, in defiance of all the etiquette of the court, to make a personal appeal to the king. Dr. Franklin, our Minister at Versailles, vehemently opposed his intention, and finding Laurens firm in his purpose, he said: " I most cordially wish you success, Colonel, but anticipate so different a result that I warn you—I wash my hands of the consequences." Accordingly, at the first levee, Colonel Laurens, walking directly up to the king, delivered a memorial, to which he solicited his most serious attention, and said: " Should the favor asked be denied, or even delayed, there is cause to fear that the sword which I wear may no longer be drawn in the defense of the liberties of my country, but be wielded as a British subject against the monarchy of France." His decision met with the reward it merited. Apologies were made for delays. The Minister gave his serious attention to the subject, and the negotiation was crowned with success.

When requested to carry a message to provost on his approach to the lines of Charleston, proposing "neutrality during the continuance of the war," he declined it with decision: " I will do anything," said he, " to serve my country, but never bear a message that would disgrace her." When General Moultrie, who equally spurned the idea of entering upon terms with the enemy, declared in council "that he would not deliver up his continentals as prisoners of war," Laurens leaped from his seat and exclaimed, "'Tis a glorious resolve General; thank God, we are on our legs again."

Had not death stopped the career of his glory he would have proven a model both of civil and military virtue, "a mirror by which our youth might dress themselves."

JOAN OF ARC.

This historic woman, known also as Jaune d'Arc and the "Maid of Orleans," was one of the most celebrated heroines of France. She was born of humble and honest parents, during the year 1412, in the village of Domremy, on the borders of Lorraine. She was the fifth child, and owing to the indigence of her father received no instruction, but was accustomed to out-of-door duties, such as the tending of sheep and the riding of horses to and from the watering places. She was taught, like other young women of her station, to spin and sew. By her modesty, greater simplicity, industry and piety, she was distinguished from the other girls of her acquaintance. When about thirteen years of age she believed that she saw a flash of light and heard an unearthly voice, which enjoined her to be modest and to be diligent in her religious duties. The impression made upon her excitable mind by the national distresses of the time, soon gave a new character to the revelation which she supposed herself to receive, and when fifteen years old she imagined that she was called to go and fight for the dauphin. Her story was at first rejected as that of an insane person. All the while she was imbibing the spirit of the times, listened to the daily and varying tale, becoming interested in political affairs. Having made her mission known to the governor, and he not being disposed to hear her at first, she was not daunted, but renewed her solicitations daily, and at each visit her importunity was increased. He at length adopted the scheme of Joan, gave her some attendants, and accompanied her to the French court.

Not the marvelous alone, but the miraculous also, is attached to the history of this extraordinary woman. An assembly of grave divines examined Joan's mission, and pronounced it to be undoubted; and the parliament, collected at Poctiers, confirmed the decisions of the theologians. Joan was dressed in a complete male suit of armor, mounted on a prancing charger, and shown to the admiring people. It was now determined to try her force against the enemy. With a sword and a white banner she put herself at the head of the French troops, whom her example and the notion of her heavenly mission inspired with new enthusiasm. On April 29, 1429, she threw herself, with supplies of provisions, into Orleans, then closely besieged by the English. and from the 4th to the 8th of May, made successful sallies upon the English, which resulted in their being compelled to raise the siege. After this important victory the national ardor of the French was rekind.ed to the utmost, and Joan became the dread of the previously triumphant English. She conducted the dauphin to Rheims, where he was crowned, July 17, 1429, and Joan, with many tears, saluted him as king. She now wished to return home, deeming her mission accomplished, but Charles importuned her to remain with his army, to which she consented.

On one occasion the French gave way, and Joan was left near'y alone. Compelled at length to join the deserters, she displayed on high the sacred banner; while with her voice, her countenance, and her gestures, she animated her recreant followers, led them back to the charge, turned the fortune of the field, and overpowered the enemy. When wounded, on another occasion, in the neck by an arrow, she retired for a moment, and exclaimed, as with her own hand she extracted the weapon, "It is glory, and not blood, which flows from this wound." The wound having been dressed quickly, she returned to head the assailants and to plant her victorious standard on the enemy's ramparts.

The English, supported by the Duke of Burgundy, laid siege to the town of Compeige, into which Joan threw herself. The garrison, who, with her assistance, believed themselves invincible, received her with transports of joy. Here, however, good fortune forsook her, and after performing prodigies of valor and losing her horse under her, she was compelled to surrender to the enemy. The Burgundians, into whose hands she had fallen, sold her to the English for ten thousand livres. It is believed the French officers, jealous of the glory of the maid, had designedly exposed her to this fatal catastrophe. Such is human gratitude and the fate of merit, and such the recompense awarded to the benefactors of their species. She was tried for sorcery and magic, and sentenced to perpetual imprisonment; and to be fed, during life, on bread and water. But the barbarous vengeance of Joan's enemies was not yet satisfied. For almost four months she was continually harrassed by questions and persecutions—the most ridiculous and absurd; she was asked whether at the coronation of Charles she had not displayed a standard consecrated by magical incantation. "Her trust," she replied, "was in the image of the Almighty impressed on the banner, and that she, who had shared the danger of the field, was entitled to partake of the glory at Rheims." During these trying examinations she betrayed no weakness, nor gave to her persecutors any advantage; she disgraced not the heroism she had displayed on the field. At length she was excommunicated, and all pardon, all mercy, refused her. Words which fell from her when subjected to great indignities, and her resumption of male attire when all articles of female dress were carefully removed from her, were made grounds of concluding that she had relapsed, and she was again brought to the stake on May 30, 1431, and burned.   On the right hand of the scaffold, on which she was exposed to the savage fury of the people, were stationed the clergy, and on the left the secular officers.   In this situation she was, with solemn mockery, interrogated on the principles of her faith, principles which appeared to differ in no respect from those of her merciless persecutors.   She was at the conclusion informed "that the meek and merciful ministers of the gospel had, for the execution of their sentence, handed her over to the secular powers."   "*Dieu soit bene !*—Blessed be God !" exclaimed the sufferer, as she placed herself on the pile.   Her body was quickly consumed and her ashes scattered to the winds.   Thus perished this heroic woman to whom "the more liberal and generous superstitions of the ancients would have erected altars."

In 1454, a revision of the sentence of Joan was demanded by her family, and the memory of Joan was fully cleared of every imputation which could tend to its dishonor.   Monuments were erected to her memory and honor in Orleans, at Rouen, and various parts of France.   The character of our subject was spotless. Her hand never shed blood.   The gentle dignity of her bearing impressed all who knew her, and restrained the brutality of her soldiers.

BENJAMIN RUST.

Self-sacrificing devotion to duty and to humanity is commendable in every age. The terrible ravages of the first appearance of the yellow fever in this country, in 1793, will never be forgotten; neither will the efforts of Benjamin Rust, whose untiring zeal was directed to allay the plague.   He certainly deserves the appellation given to St. Luke, of "the beloved physician."   He was born near Philadelphia, Dec. 24, 1745, and was educated at Princeton college.   He was elected a member of the continental congress and advocated and signed the declaration of independence.   He received several high appointments, although he saw fit to refuse many others.   He cared not to act in public capacities, preferring rather to occupy the more humble walks of life.   He resigned his post in the army, because he could not prevent frauds upon the soldiers in the hospital stores.   In 1785, he planned the Philadelphia dispensary, the first in the United States.   It is believed that he saved the lives of 6,000 persons during the yellow fever epidemic.   When many alarmed physicians fled, Dr. Rust remained at the post of duty, with a few faithful students.   Some of his pupils died, and he was violently attacked by the disease, yet he did not remit his labors when he could leave his bed.   In all stations he exhibited the character of a consistent Christian, and his principles remained unscathed amid all the infidelity which French writers had infused into the minds of men in high places toward the close of the last century.   That great and good man died peacefully at Philadelphia, on the 19th of April, 1813, when in the sixty-eighth year of his age.

HANNAH DUSTIN.

"Experience teaches us that resolution's a sole help at need:"

The pioneer women of this country found it necessary to be bold in every enterprise. When the Indians who dwelt at the source of the Merrimac River and in the region around about, after a great freshet on the fifteenth of March, 1697, came down the river and attacked Haverhill, Hannah Dustin was confined to her bed with an infant only a week old. Her husband catching the alarm from the field fled to the house and consulted his wife on the course he should pursue. She calmly told him to leave her and her infant to their fate, and to make his escape, if possible, with her other children. He sent seven of the children on a path through the woods, on the way to the garrison, and mounting

MRS. DUSTIN'S MIDNIGHT ATTACK.

his horse he followed in the rear; with his musket he kept the pursuing Indians at bay, until he found his charge in a safe place. Before Mr. Dustin reached the garrison, the Indians returned and captured his sick wife and Mary Neif, her nurse. They, with other captives, took up their march by order of the savages, for the north. After they had traveled a few miles, the Indians found the infant troublesome, and taking the child from the arms of the nurse, dashed its brains out against a tree. Mrs. Dustin was feeble and wretched, but this outrage nerved her soul for every enterprise. She wept no more; the agony of nature drank the tear-drop ere it fell. She looked to heaven with a silent prayer for succor and vengeance, and followed the infernal group without a word of complaint. They were marched through the wilderness for several days, till they came to a halt on an island in the Merrimac river, about six miles above Concord, New Hampshire. There they were placed in a wigwam occupied by two men, three women, seven children of theirs, and an English boy who had been captured about a year previous, at Worcester. The captives remained there till the thirtieth of the month before they planned escape. On that day the boy was requested by Mrs. Dustin to ask his master where to strike "to kill instantly," and the savage was simple enough to tell, and also instructed him in the art of scalping. "At night, while the household slumbers, the captives, each with a tomahawk, strike vigorously and fleetly, and with division of labor—and of the twelve sleepers, ten lie dead; of one squaw the wound was not mortal; one child was spared from design. The love of glory next asserted its power; and the gun and tomahawk of the murderer of her infant, and a bag heaped full of scalps, were choicely kept as trophies of the heroine. The streams are the guides which God has set for the stranger in the wilderness; in a bark canoe the three descended the Merrimac to the English settlements, astonishing their friends by their escape, and filling the land with wonder at their successful daring." Mrs. Dustin had the happiness of meeting her husband and seven children, who had escaped from the house before the savages entered, and the honor of a very handsome present from Colonel Nicholson, governor of Maryland, as a reward for her heroism. The people of Boston made her many presents. All classes were anxious to see the heroine, and they found her as modest as brave.

DIXON H. LEWIS.

Ample as were the bodily dimensions of Senator Lewis, of Alabama, they were but a true indication of the greatness of his mind. An anecdote is told of him which is a characteristic one. Upon his return from Washington, at one time, the vessel in which he had embarked was overtaken by a storm, which so damaged her timbers that she was soon found to be in a sinking condition. The safety of the passengers and crew depended on the long boat, to which they had recourse, and she was loaded to the water's edge. Mr. Lewis was the last person on board the sinking ship, and as he was about to leave her he saw the perilous condition of the boat which his weight, for he exceeded four hundred pounds must inevitably swamp, and he positively refused to enter until she had been to land and deposited her living freight safe on shore. It was a question of one life against many. If he entered the boat all might be lost, while he alone would sink with the ship if he were not rescued before she went down; and he generously and heroically resigned himself to what appeared to be inevitable destruction that he might save his fellow passengers. He was, however, happily saved, and long afterward represented his state in the United States Senate.

A GIRL'S HEROISM.

Remarkable instances of deeds of daring and heroism are by no means scarce in which children occupy the commendable roles. Great presence of mind was exhibited by a little girl of Picton, South Carolina. She was only seven years old, and was with her brother, aged five years, locked up by her mother on going out. Some female wearing apparel took fire from a lamp. Alice, the little girl, knew that the key was left in the door outside. She formed the terrible project of jumping from the third story window, and thus releasing her brother. Lowering herself by the arms as far as possible, she dropped a distance of thirty-five feet. Her clothes buoyed her up, and she was not much injured. But when she rushed up to the chamber door and opened it, her brother was gone. He, too, had crawled out of the window to see where his sister had gone, and fell to the ground. He was somewhat scratched, but not seriously injured. An arm and leg of the daring girl were hurt, but not seriously.

SAMUEL KIRKLAND.

Peerless among those faithful messengers who carried the gospel of peace, love and brotherhood to the dark minded without the pale of civilization, was Samuel Kirkland; who, for forty years labored with untiring zeal among the pagans of central New York. He was born at Norwich, Connecticut, on the 1st of December, 1741, and through life exhibited the indomitable courage, energy and perseverance of his Scotch lineage. In Dr. Wheelock's school, which he had entered to prepare to be a missionary among the Indians, he was much beloved for his gentleness; a quality which endeared him to his fellow students at Princeton. He entered upon this work and made his residence among the Oneidas at their council house, a little south-west of Fort Stanoix, now Rome. There he built a house with his own hands, and labored day and night for the good of the poor Indians. Toil and exposure impaired his health. During all the troubles and insecurities of those times, he did not desert his post, but labored on through all the dark scenes of the seven year's war that ensued, not only for the spiritual benefit of the dusky tribes, but in unceasing endeavors to keep the six nations neutral. He accompanied a delegation of Senecas to Philadelphia, in 1790, and was rewarded by the conversion of the great chief, Cornplanter, with whom he traveled, instructed and convinced. In 1793, he established an institution of learning, under the title of *The Hamilton Oneida Academy*. This was the origin of Hamilton College. Up to the time of his death, in 1808, when he was in the sixty-seventh year of his age, he continued his self-sacrificing work among the Oneidas. His life is a beautiful example of Christian purity and devotion to the cause of enlightening the darkened minds of the savages.

JAMES MILNOR.

It has been the privilege of very few men to be so eminently useful as James Milnor, in all that pertains to the well being of his fellow creatures. In the domestic circle, he was reverenced for his unalloyed goodness; in the legal profession he was called "the honest lawyer;" as a legislator he was beneficent and patriotic; as a Christian he was without guile; and in the Protestant Episcopal Church, he was one of the most prominent of all her evangelical clergy; yet in nothing wanting as one of her most loyal sons.

He was early sent to college; but to relieve his father of heavy expenses on his account, James left the university before taking his degree, and at the age of about sixteen years commenced the study of law. At one time, when a member of congress, Henry Clay, then the speaker, becoming incensed at one of Milnor's debates, challenged him to a duel. Mr. Milnor bravely refused, first because Mr. Clay had no right to call him to account for his public acts, and secondly because he was opposed, in principle, to the cowardly practice of dueling. There the matter ended, and in after years, when Mr. Milnor was an eminent minister of the Gospel, he and the great statesman met on the most friendly terms. On one of his visits home, during his term in congress, his little daughter, Anna, met him as he entered the house, and said: " Papa, do you know I can read?" "No, let me hear you," he replied. She selected the words, " Thou shalt love the Lord thy God with all thy heart." This incident made a great impression on his mind. Religious truths were pressed upon his mind, and he changed from his original profession to that of the ministry. His ministerial career was brilliant. Dr. Milnor was extremely active in the promotion of schemes of Christian benevolence. He was one of the founders of the American Tract Society, in 1824, and continued to be one of its most active members until his death. The Institution for the Deaf and Dumb, the Orphan Asylum, the Home for aged indigent females, and many kindred institutions, felt his fostering care. His whole life was spent in doing good; and when death came, he departed knowing that he had left as a legacy a life well spent.

ZACHARY TAYLOR.

The people of the United States are professedly peace-loving, yet nowhere is a military hero more sincerely worshiped by vast masses than here; not, we may charitably hope, because of his vocation, but because of the good achieved for his country by his brave deeds; and when that worship is excessive because of some brilliant act, then the people desire to apotheosize the hero by crowning him with the highest honors of the nation—the civic wreath of chief magistrate. When war was declared against Great Britain in 1812, Zachary Taylor held a captain's commission, and he was placed in command of Fort Harrison, a stockade on the Wabash River. There, in his gallant operations against the Indians, he gave promise of future renown, and for his heroic defense of his post he was breveted major. He served with distinction under General Scott in the "Black Hawk war." Then he went to Florida, and in his operations against the Seminoles he evinced generalship superior to any officer there. He was actively engaged in the Mexican war; and on his return he was greeted everywhere with the wildest enthusiasm. For his daring intrepidity and unwavering courage, the Whig party, governed by the applauding voice of the nation, regarded him as eminently "available," and nominated him for the office of President of the United States. He was elected by a large majority; but the duties of his office bore heavily upon him, and after holding the reins of the federal government for sixteen months, death came to the presidential mansion, and on the 9th of July, 1850, the brave hero died, at the age of sixty-five years.

ANNE BOLEYN.

"Uneasy rests the head that wears a crown," was never better verified than in the life of the subject of this sketch.

Anne Boleyn was born in 1507, and carried to France at seven years of age. After the death of Louis his widow returned to her native country, but Anne remained in France. The beauty and accomplishments of Anne attracted, even at a very early age, general admiration at the French court. She returned to England about the time when scruples were first entertained by Henry VIII. respecting the legality of his marriage with the betrothed wife and widow of his brother, Catharine of Arragon. In his visits to the queen, to whom Anne Boleyn became maid of honor, Henry had an opportunity of observing her beauty and captivating manner. Anne quickly perceived her influence over the heart of the monarch, whose passion, either from principle or policy, she resolutely resisted. The enamored Henry, despairing of succeeding with the lady but upon honorable terms, was, by her conduct, stimulated to redouble his efforts to procure a release from his former engagements. The impatience of Henry suffered him not to wait for a dissolution of his marriage with Catharine; a private ceremony united him with Anne Boleyn on the 14th of November, 1532. The marriage was made public on Easter eve, 1533, when Anne was declared queen of England and crowned the first of the following June.

The affection of the king for his new queen seemed, for a time, to increase rather than diminish by possession, but in about six years his love began to languish and visibly decay. The enemies of Anne, who were the first to perceive the change, eagerly sought to widen the breach, and jealousy was the engine which they employed for her destruction, with the greatest success. No real stigma has been thrown on the conduct of Anne, but a certain levity of spirits and gayety of character, which she had probably acquired from her education in France, rendered her manners unguarded. She was more vain than proud, and took a coquettish pleasure in beholding the effects of her charms, and indulged herself in an easy familiarity with those who had formerly been her equals. Her popular manners offended the dignity of Henry; if the lover had been blind to the foibles of his mistress, the husband became but too quick sighted to the indiscretions of his wife. A passion for a new object had vanquished, in the heart of a capricious despot, the small remains of his affection for Anne, who was supplanted in the affections of her husband. His jealousy, over which he secretly brooded, first manifested itself at a tournament at Greenwich, where the queen having let fall her handkerchief, he construed this accident into a signal of gallantry, and retiring instantly from the place sent orders to confine her to her chamber. Five gentlemen, charged with being her paramours, were arrested and thrown into prison. She was the next day sent to the Tower, and on her way thither informed of what she had till then been unconscious, the crimes and misdemeanor alleged against her. As she entered the prison she fell on her knees and called God to witness how guiltless she was of the offenses imputed to her charge.

The sweetness and beneficence of Anne's temper had, during her prosperity, made her numberless friends, but in her falling fortunes no one even attempted to interpose between her and the fury of the king; she, whose appearance had dressed every face in smiles, was now abandoned, unpitied and alone, to her adverse destiny.

The gentlemen who were imprisoned on her account, although no proof of their gu lt was made out, were condemned and executed. The queen and her brother, the Viscount Rocheford, were tried by a jury of peers. Anne, though unassisted by counsel, defended herself with so much clearness and presence of mind that the spectators unanimously believed her to be guiltless. Judgment was, however, passed by the court both against her and her brother. She was sentenced by the verdict to be beheaded or burned, according to the king's pleasure. "Oh! Father," said she, lifting up her eyes, when this dreadful sentence was pronounced, "Oh! Creator, thou who art the way, the truth, and the life, thou knowest that I have not deserved this death!" Then turning to the judges she pathetically declared her innocence. In her last message to the king she thanked him for having advanced her from private life to the throne, and now since he could raise her no higher in this word he was sending her to heaven. She earnestly recommended her daughter to his care, and renewed her protestations of her innocence and fidelity. At the scaffold she prayed for the king, and said to the lieutenant of the Tower, "The executioner is, I hear, very expert, and my neck," grasping it with her hand, and laughing heartily, "is very slender." She met death with firmness, and her body was thrown negligently into a common elm chest, made to hold arrows, and buried in the Tower.

REWARD OF A BRAVE DEED.

Every year on the occasion of the national fetes the Belgian government makes a public distribution of rewards to persons who have performed remarkable acts of courage in good causes. Among those who were rewarded recently was a little boy of nine, whose exploit may be contrasted with the behavior of the people who allowed the little girl to be drowned in Kensington Gardens. Genin, playing in a field a few months ago, saw a little girl fall into the Sambre. Without knowing who the child was, he plunged into the river, and after some trouble saved her. The child turned out to be his own sister. Not content with having rescued her from death, Genin, like a good-hearted little boy, wanted to shield her from the punishment she had deserved for playing too near the river, contrary to her parents' orders. So he took the blame of her disobedience upon himself and received a beating from his father. The little girl, however, could not bear to see him suffer in this way, and afterward told the whole truth, which was corroborated by the evidence of an eye witness. The facts then became public, and young Genin was summoned to Brussels at the fetes to receive a national recompense. He was of course loudly cheered as he stepped up to the platform, and M. Rolin-Jacquemyns, the Home Minister, in pinning a medal to his breast, called him a little hero.

ROBERT MORRIS.

To the zeal and ability of Washington alone, were superior honors due, than to Robert Morris, whose extraordinary powers in the Department of Finance, and successful exertions in the accomplishment of our independence every historian cannot but laud. At the time when the army of Washington was perplexed and dismayed, having neither ammunition or money to purchase the same, when the spouts of houses were melted to furnish lead, Morris had landed a vessel with ninety tons of lead, the half of which fortunate supply he gave to the war officers, and prevailed upon his partners to give the other half also. The firm of which he was a member were among the most wealthy importers of Philadelphia, and consequently they were the heaviest losers by the non-importation agreements, which gave such a deadly blow at the infant commerce of the colonies, after the passage of the stamp act. Yet they patriotically joined the league, and made the sacrifice for the good of the cause of right. In November, 1775, Mr. Morris was elected to a seat in the continental congress, where his exceeding great usefulness was soon discovered. Toward the close of the year 1776, when the half naked, half famished American army were about to cease the struggle in despair, he evinced his faith in the success of the conflict, and his own warm patriotism by loaning for the government, on his own responsibility, ten thousand dollars. "I want money," said Morris to a Quaker friend, "for the use of the army." "What security canst thou give?" asked the lender. "My note and my honor," responded Morris. "Robert, thou shalt have it," was the prompt reply. It gave food and clothing to the gallant little band under Washington, who achieved the noble victory at Trenton, and a new and powerful impetus was thereby given to the revolution. He submitted a plan and established the bank of North America, in 1781, with a capital of $400,000, which was of great use to the government.

He was a senator in the first congress convened under the Federal Constitution, and Washington appointed him First Secretary of the Treasury. At the close of his senatorial term, Mr. Morris retired from public life, not so rich in money, by half, as when he entered the arena. Soon the remainder of his fortune was lost in wild land speculations. On the 8th of May, 1806, Robert Morris, the great financier of the revolution, died in comparative poverty, at the age of seventy-three years. He had husbanded, and with success, the funds of the public, but dissipated his own.

JOHN EDWARDS.

It must appear both injudicious and unjust that Mr. John Edwards has been so little noticed. This name has been scarcely mentioned in the records of our revolution; yet, there was no citizen of the republic in whose bosom the love of liberty glowed with more generous enthusiasm. Possessing wealth beyond any other mercantile man of the day, he was the first individual in Carolina who tendered his fortunes in support of the American cause. Warned by his more prudential friends that he placed to much at hazard; that the success of America, opposed to the power of Britain, could scarcely be expected, and that the total loss of his ample possessions might follow, with a feeling of patriotism that cannot be too highly appreciated, he replied: "Be it so! I would rather lose my all than retain it, subject to British authority." His subsequent conduct gives ample testimony that this was no vain boasting. When reprimanded by friends, that his course was impolitic and would bring odium upon his name, Mr. Edwards said: "Admiral Arbuthnot, it is not the temptation of wealth that shall ever induce me to forfeit my honor. I cannot hesitate to choose, where duty, inclination, and every virtuous principle point out the course which it becomes me to pursue. My losses have been great, but they cost me not a sigh. My moneys were lent to support a cause which I consider that of justice and humanity. I have a wife, tenderly beloved, and ten children worthy of my most ardent affection. They are all dependent on me, and I may probably have little to leave them but good principles and an untarnished reputation; but, were a gallows to be raised by your order, in my view, and you were to say—*Your fate depends upon your resolve—take protection or perish*—I would, without a moment's hesitation—*die!*"

His brave and heroic life must be admired when it is remembered that, hearing in council the magnanimous proposition to await the event of an assault and to devote the lives of the garrison at Charleston to the attainment of general good, rather than surrender to the enemy, he nobly supported the opinion, and heroically declared for death in preference to submission. "I would rather," he exclaimed, "that my breast should meet the British bayonet, than that my signature should be given to any proposition recommending the surrender of the city."

PHEBE ABBOT.

"One grain of incense with devotion offered,
Is beyond all perfumes or sabean spices."
—*Massinger*.

Time has not been able to eradicate the noble life of Phebe Abbot, the wife of Captain Henry Abbot, of Andover, in Massachusetts. Her husband was a fine specimen of the commonwealths-men of those days. Mrs. Abbot managed her household affairs with great exactness and economy, but still with liberality. Not a crumb was lost, nor an ingredient misapplied. She had not a large family of her own, only two sons and a daughter; and the eldest son was not much at home, having been educated at Harvard University. But their large farm and mansion house was fitted up for boarders. Students of the Phillips Academy, to the number of half a dozen or more, were accommodated here. No fond mother could be more attentive to the health, morals, and habits of her offspring than Mrs. Abbot was to those under her care. The household affairs were all managed without bustle, that no boy might plead the excuse that he was interrupted in his studies by the noise of the spinning wheel or the churn. She and her husband were members of the Congregational church in the place, and were as regular as the holy Sabbath came, at divine service; and every boy was required to be in readiness to attend her to her place of worship; and there the slightest misconduct or neglect was noticed and reproved. Time passed on and seasons changed; but nothing but death made changes in her arrangements. Mrs. Abbot was a woman of a strong mind, which was most admirably disciplined; of excellent principles, of great equanimity of temper, and of fine health; always at or near home, ready for every care which her family demanded. Such a woman was a good guide to youth; and she read their characters at a glance. She excited her boys to study, and felt as delighted as a mother when they won testimonials of improvement. On such occasions some little nicety was provided for them to show that she had an interest in their reputation. She had the misfortune to lose her only daughter, when full grown, and just entering into life with fair prospects; but even this calamity did not disturb her composure. "The Lord gave and the Lord hath taken away; blessed be his name;" was all that escaped her lips under this bereavement. Nature had done much toward making her a woman of fortitude, but religion had done more. In the summer of 1833, at the ripe old age of eighty-seven years, she died. For a few years before her death she had been afflicted with blindness; but this did not change her temper. She said that the great Disposer of events had done all this to detach her from the world, and to teach her to contemplate the great change about to take place. If it gave permanent glory in Rome to have educated two bright boys, what honor belongs to her, who had during her prilgrimage, more than two hundred under her maternal care, and all of them having cause for blessing her name. It requires wisdom to direct minds, and it is proof of virtue to have educated others to good habits. If the mothers of our country cannot boast of the glories of fashion, or their taste in the arts, it must be acknowledged that those virtues which give strength to principles and security to society are eminently theirs. It is not in the higher regions of life that its value can be truly ascertained. The elevated must act for others as well as themselves; those depressed below the ordinary level of existence have seldom sufficient fortitude to see all the bearings of human duties. It is in the more common walks of society that the true nature of man is best ascertained; those who have neither poverty nor riches have few temptations.

BENJAMIN FRANKLIN.

On the 17th of January, 1706, the subject of this sketch was born. At the age of eight years he went to a grammar school, but at ten his services were required in his father's business, and his education was neglected. He afterward became an apprentice in his brother's printing office, and a love for reading was gratified, often at the expense of half a night's sleep. He contributed some articles to his brother's paper which attracted attention, although the author was unsuspected. He became a skeptic in religion, and a powerful disputant. Leaving Boston, he went to New York, and from there to Philadelphia, where he soon procured employment as a printer. With promises of aid from Governor Keith, he left for London, to purchase printing material for the purpose of beginning business for himself. The aid was withheld, and he was compelled to seek employment for a livelihood. By practicing strict economy he saved the greater part of his wages; and his influence among his fellow workmen against useless expenses for beer and other things was beneficial. At night he used his pen, and wrote strongly in favor of infidelity. In after years the early efforts of his pen in opposition to Christian ethics were looked upon by him with much regret. In 1726 he returned once more to Philadelphia, again being employed by Mr. Keimer. His ingenuity was profitable to his employer, for he engraved devices on type metal, made printers' ink, and in various ways saved money to the establishment. He subsequently purchased a newspaper, opened a stationery store, formed a literary club, and laid the foundation of the Public Library of Philadelphia. All the while he was becoming more popular in the province. The fact is demonstrated by the circumstance that by his personal exertions he obtained ten thousand names to a voluntary association for the defense of the province in 1744, when an attempt to procure a militia law had failed. Franklin's electrical experiments, and the results of the same, are revolutionary in their nature; and by the coincident of an iron-pointed kite flying in a storm, and similar points fastened to buildings, established the proof of his lightning-rod theory. During the whole period of the revolution he was continually active in a civil capacity at home or abroad. In the mind of Franklin the love for union assumed majestic proportions, and comprehended the great country back of the Apalachian mountains. "In less than a century," said he, with the gift of prophecy, "it must undoubtedly become a populous and powerful dominion." The freedom of the American colonies, their union, and their extension through the west, became the three great objects of the remaining years of Franklin.

Heaven, in its mercy, gave the illustrious statesman length of days, so that he lived to witness the fulfillment of his hopes in all their grandeur.

On the 17th of April, 1790, that great philosopher, statesman and sage, was undressed for the grave; and beneath a neat marble slab, in the burial ground of Christ Church, Philadelphia, rest his mortal remains. In all his labors Franklin was ever actuated by an intense desire to promote the well-being and happiness of his fellow men; and few have been more successful in their aims. From poverty he rose to wealth, and from ignorance and obscurity to extensive erudition and honorable renown, gaining for himself the admiration of Europe and the gratitude of America. The one grand lesson and object of his life was not to shut his heart against private friendships. He loved his family and his friends, and was extremely beneficent. In society he was sententious, but not fluent; a listener rather than a talker; an informant rather than a pleasing companion. Impatient of interruption, he often mentioned the custom of the Indians, who always remain silent some time before they give an answer to a question, which they have heard attentively—unlike some of the politest societies in Europe, where a sentence can scarcely be finished without interruption. He made various bequests and donations to cities, public bodies, and individuals.

DAVID GLASCOE FARRAGUT.

"I have no volition in the matter; your duty is to give orders, mine to obey." So wrote Commandant Farragut to the secretary of the navy, in 1856, on receiving an intimation from him that if he would indicate his preference for a station, it would be granted. This sentence is a key to his whole public character, from his entrance into the navy as midshipman before he was ten years of age. He was born near Knoxville, Tenn., July 5th, 1801. His father was a native of Minorca, and came to America in 1776, when he became an active soldier in the continental army. His early life was passed on the frontier. Capt. David Porter took charge of him when he was between nine and ten years of age, and on December 17th, 1810, he was appointed a midshipman. He first served on the *Essex*, under Porter, and was with him on his long cruise to the Pacific ocean in 1812-13. Porter entrusted him with the command of a prize to be taken into Valparaiso, while he was yet a little boy. "I was sent as prize-master to the *Barclay*," wrote Farragut in after years. "This was an important event in my life, and when it was decided that I was to take the ship to Valparaiso, I felt no little pride at finding myself in command at twelve years of age. He was engaged in the battle between the *Essex* and the *Phœbe* and *Cherub*, off Valparaiso. Capt. Farragut was put in a very delicate position on the breaking out of the civil war. By nativity and by marriage of two wives in succession, he was identified with the slave-labor states. When his country was assailed by its recreant children in the southern states, and scores of southern-born naval officers deserted the old flag and joined the enemies of the republic, Farragut did not hesitate a moment in choosing to defend the union, for he was a true patriot, owing his allegiance to the national government, not to the pretended petty sovereignty of a state. He took his family to a village on the Hudson River, and then went forth to give mighty blows against the dragon of rebellion. All through the four years' war that ensued he was the model commander wherever his flag was seen, whether on the Mississippi River or the gulf of Mexico, in his good wooden ship *Hartford.* He led in the expedition for the capture of New Orleans, and in efforts to make the Mississippi River free for the navigation of national vessels. He attempted to reduce Vicksburg, and took a conspicuous part in the attack on Port Hudson, the following year. For his services at New Orleans, and on the Mississippi River above and below, he was thanked by congress, and placed first on the list of rear-admirals soon afterward created. He did gallant service on the coast of Texas, as commander of the Gulf squadron. His most brilliant achievement during the war was in Mobile Bay, near the close of the summer of 1864. Lashed to a position among the shrouds of the *Hartford,* where he could oversee and command his whole squadron, he boldly sailed into the bay, fighting a fort, gun-boats, and a powerful ram, and every moment in danger of destruction by torpedoes. One of these destroyed an iron-clad gun-boat just in front of the *Hartford.* She filled and sank in a few seconds, carrying down her commander and nearly all of her men. At that moment he felt that all was lost, but his first impulse was to appeal to heaven for guidance, and he prayed; "Oh, God, who created man and gave him reason, direct me what to do. Shall I go on?" And it seemed as if a voice in answer commanded him to "Go on!" and he cried out: "Four bells! Capt. Drayton, go ahead! Jouett, full speed!" and victory was the result.

A BENEVOLENT WIDOW.

Several years ago, a poor widow had placed a smoked herring—the last morsel of food she had in the house—on the table for herself and children, when a stranger entered and solicited food, saying that he had had nothing to eat for twenty-four hours. The widow hesitatingly offered to share the herring with him, remarking, at the same time, "We shall not be forsaken or suffer deeper for an act of charity." As the stranger drew near the table and saw the scantiness of the fare, he asked, "Is this all your store? Do you offer a share to one you do not know? Then I never saw charity before. But, madam, do you not wrong your children by giving a part of your morsel to a stranger?" "Ah," said she, with tears in her eyes, "I have a boy, a darling son, somewhere on the face of the wide world—unless heaven has taken him away—and I only act toward you as I would that others should act toward him. God, who sent manna from heaven, can provide for us as he did for Israel; and how should I this night offend him, if my son should be a wanderer, destitute as you, and he should have provided for him a home, even as poor as this, were I to turn you unrelieved away." The stranger whom she thus addressed was the long absent son to whom she referred; and when she stopped speaking he sprang from his feet, clasped her in his arms, and exclaimed, "God, indeed, has provided just such a home for your wandering son, and has given him wealth to reward the goodness of his benefactress. My mother! Oh, my mother!"

STEPHEN VAN RENSSELAER.

"He was one of the best men of his time, in the highest sense of t c term." When war was declared against Great Britain, in 1812, Mr. Van Rensselaer having the commission of major-general, was placed by Governor Tompkins in command of the New York militia destined for the defense of the northern frontier. After the war, when in the federal congress, by casting his vote, he gave the presidency of the United States to John Quincy Adams. With that session closed the political life of this great man, but he still labored on and hoped on in the higher sphere of duty of a benevolent Christian. Like his Master, whom he loved, he was ever "meek and lowly," and "went about doing good." He did not wait for misery to call at his door; he sought out the children of want; to the poor and ignorant he was a blessing. In 1824 he founded a seminary for the purpose of "qualifying teachers for instructing the children of farmers and mechanics in the application of experimental chemistry, philosophy, and natural history, to agriculture, domestic economy, the arts and manufactures. He liberally endowed it, and the "*Rensselaer School*" is a perpetual hymn to the memory and praise of its benefactor. In the cause of the bible, temperance, and every social and moral reform, Mr. Van Rensselaer's time and money were freely given, and in these labors he continued until death.

ABIGAIL ADAMS.

There are few lives that will bear the scrutinizing gaze of a critic to examine the every-day life and actions, as they are exhibited to the world around. Fewer still, that will admit of an examination of the inmost recesses of the heart, and permit all the hopes and feelings to be laid bare; such a life, however, was that of ,Abigail Adams, wife of John Adams. When the world is permitted to study such a life, it always concludes that "great minds like heaven, are pleased in doing good."

Abigail Smith—afterward Mrs. Adams—was the daughter of Rev. William Smith, a Congregational minister, of Weymouth, Massachusetts, where she was born on the 11th of November, 1744. "It was fashionable to ridicule female learning," in her day; and she says of herself in one of her letters, "I was never sent to any school; I was always sick. Female education in the best families wènt no further than writing and arithmetic." But notwithstanding her educational disadvantages, she read and studied in private, and kept up a brisk correspondence with relatives, and by this means expanded and fed her mind, and cultivated an easy and graceful style of writing. Few women of the present day are so well acquainted with the standard English authors. The personal and mental accomplishments of this young lady attracted the attention and secured the affection of Mr. Adams, then a young man of distinction at the bar in Massachusetts. They were married in 1764, and resided in Boston. The first ten years of Mrs. Adams' married life were passed in a quiet and happy manner, her enjoyment suffering no interruptions except those occasioned by the short absences of her husband when he attended the courts. In this period she became the mother of a daughter and three sons, of whom John Quincy Adams was the eldest.

In 1778 Mr. Adams was sent to France as a joint commissioner. While he was absent from his country on that occasion, faithful to the call of duty, his wife remained at home and managed, as she had done before, the affairs of the farm and household. And *there* let the reader look at her and see a picture of a true mother of the Revolution. "She is a farmer, cultivating the land, and discussing the weather and crops; a merchant reporting price-current and the rates of exchange, and directing the making up of invoices; a politician, speculating upon the probabilities of peace or war; and a mother, writing the most exalted sentiments to her son." Those were perilous moments; the wise were baffled by the outlook and prospect of war; the courageous hesitated, and the great mass of the people were inflamed but confused; they had no fixed and settled purpose, but all was left for the development of time. Mr. Adams was one of the boldest in the march of honest resistance to tyranny. To Mrs. Adams he communicated his thoughts freely on all the high matters of state, for he had the fullest confidence in her fortitude, prudence, secrecy, and good sense, without the test which the Roman Portia gave her lord, to gain his cofidence in matters of policy, 'when the state was out of joint.' In the midst of her public cares and anxieties, she did not neglect her sacred duties as a mother. The care of the education of her four children devolved entirely upon her. This subject occupied much of her attention; and, indeed, the greatest value of her published correspondence consists in the hints which it gives us of the course of culture pursued in producing those glorious fruits, of which other generations have had the enjoyment. She carefully guarded against the contagion of vice at that period when the mind and heart are most susceptible to impressions. "I have always thought it," she says to her husband, "of very great importance that children should, in the early part of life, be accustomed to such examples as would tend to corrupt the purity of their words and actions, that they may chill with horror at the sound of an oath, and blush with indignation at an obscene expression. These first principles, which grow with their growth, and strengthen with their strength, neither time nor custom can totally eradicate." Can we be surprised at the abhorrence which her "illustrious son of an illustrious mother" ever exhibited to oppression, when we find her thus expressing her sentiments in behalf of the oppressed, at a time when the subject of which she speaks had not excited any attention either in Europe or America? "I wish sincerely that there was not a slave in the province; it always appeared to me a most iniquitous scheme to fight ourselves for what we are daily robbing from those who have as good a right to freedom as we have." When Mr. Adams was chosen vice-president, she was the same unaffected, intelligent, and elegant woman. No little managements, no private views, no sly interferences with public affairs, was ever for a moment charged to her. When her husband became chief magistrate, the widest field opened for the exercise of all the talent and acquirements of Mrs. Adams; and her fondest admirers were not disappointed. She graced the table by her courtesy and elegance of manners, and delighted her guests by the powers of her conversation. But this was not all; her acquaintance with public affairs, her discrimination of character, her discernment of the signs of the times, and her pure patriotism, made her an excellent cabinet minister; and, to the honor of her husband, he never forgot nor undervalued her worth. The politicians of that period speak with enthusiasm of her foresight, her prudence, and the wisdom of her observations. Tracy respected, Bayard admired, and Ames eulogized her; all parties had the fullest confidence in the purity of her motives and in the elevation of her understanding. Fatigue and anguish often overwhelmed the president, from the weight and multiplicity of his labors and cares; but her sensibility, affection, and cheerfulness, chased the frown from his brow, and plucked the root of bitterness from his heart.

Peremptory denial produces enmity and confusion, but gentle evasion and cautious replies soften the hearts of the restless, and temper the passions of the sanguine. An intelligent woman can control these repinings and hush these murmurings with much less sacrifice or effort than men. Mrs. Adams calmed these agitations of disappointment, healed the rankling wound of offended pride, and left men in admiration of her talents and in love with her sincerity. Notwithstanding these numerous duties and great exertions, as the wife of a statesman, Mrs. Adams did not forget that she was a parent; she prided herself in her children, although she did not make the boast of Graechi. Many women fill important stations with the most splendid display of virtues, but few are equally great in retirement; there they want the animating influence of a thousand eyes, and the inspiration of homage and flattery; this is human nature in its common forms and the exception is honorable and rare. From her husband's retirement from the presidency, in 1801, to the close of her life, in 1818, Mrs. Adams remained constantly at Quincy, cheerful, contented, and happy. She devoted her last years in that rural seclusion to the reciprocities of friendship and love, to the offices of kindness and charity, and in short, to all duties which tend to ripen the Christian for an exchange of worlds. Her influence over Mr. Adams was remarkable, and she must have much of the credit of making him what he was. Mr. Adams himself wrote: "Upon examining the biography of illustrious men, you will generally find some female about them, in the relation of mother, or wife, or sister, to whose instigation a great part of their merit is to be ascribed. You will find a curious example of this in the case of Aspasia, the wife of Pericles. She taught him, it is said, his refined maxims of policy, his lofty imperial eloquence; nay, even composed his speeches on which so great a share of his reputation was founded." Mr. Adams had such a wife, and he owed his greatness to _his_ Aspasia. The exalted patriotism and the cheerful piety infused into the letters she addressed to him during the long nights of political uncertainty that hung over the colonies, strengthened his courage, fired his nobler feelings, nerved his higher purposes, and, doubtless, greatly contributed to make him the right-hand man of Washington. Serenity, purity, and the elevation of thought, preserve the faculties of the mind from permanent decay, and, indeed, keep them vigorous in old age; to such, the lapse of time is only the change of the shadow on the dial of life. The diligent and faithful Andromachs, the gifted and patriotic Aspasias of the Revolution, did their portion of the great work silently and unseen; secretly they urged their husbands and sons to the battle-field, secretly spoke to them by letter in the camp or convention, and secretly prayed for wisdom to guide our statesmen and victory to crown our arms. Thus privately acting, how little of their labor or their worth is known. How few of their names are treasured in our annals; with rare exceptions—like the builders of the pyramids—their initials are lost. Then, while we have the name and the noble example of Mrs. Adams—with a few of her patriotic compeers—let us pledge our unswerving devotion to Freedom, over the _unknown_ names of the wives and mothers who secretly assisted in nerving the arm that broke the scepter of British dominion on these shores, and gave the eagle of Liberty a safe and abiding home on the mountain tops. She lived long enough to see the seeds of virtue and knowledge which she had planted in the minds of her children, spring up and ripen into maturity; to receive a recompense in addition to the consciousness of duty performed, for her anxiety and labors, in the respect and honors which her eldest son received from his countrymen. And " to live in hearts we leave behind, is not to die."

JAMES EDWARD OGLETHORPE.

A philanthropist, coming to our beautiful land for the purpose of perfecting a benevolent scheme which his tender heart and sound judgment had conceived, was James E. Oglethorpe. To him, in the annals of legislative philanthropy, the honor is due of having first resolved to redress the griefs that had so long been immured from the public gaze—to lighten the lot of debtors. Touched with the sorrows which the walls of a prison could not hide from his merciful eye, he searched into the gloomy horrors of jails,

" Where sickness pines, where thirst and hunger burn,
And poor misfortune feels the lash of vice."

While a representative in Parliament, in 1728, he was placed upon a committee to inquire into the condition of imprisoned debtors in Great Britain. His benevolent heart was pained at the recitals of woe that fell upon his ears. The virtuous and the good were alike cast into loathsome prisons. He submitted a plan for establishing a military colony south of the Savannah River, as a barrier between the Carolinians and the Spaniards in Florida, to be composed of the virtuous debtors then in prison throughout the kingdom. Here former poverty would be no reproach, and the simplicity of piety could indulge the spirit of devotion without fear of persecution from men who hated the rebuke of its example. A royal charter for twenty-one years was granted to a corporation "in trust for the poor," to establish a colony to be called Georgia, in honor of King George the Second. In the prosecution of his benevolent enterprise he crossed the ocean several times. Spanish jealousy finally becoming aroused, Oglethorpe built forts and protected his rapidly growing colony, and gave it permanency. When General Gage, who was governor of Massachusetts and commander-in-chief of the British forces in America, went to England in 1775, the supreme command in this country was offered to Oglethorpe. The merciful conditions upon which alone he would accept the appointment did not please the ministry, and General Howe was sent. He was eulogized by Pope, Dr. Johnson and Thomson, who regarded him as possessing the highest philanthropic virtues.

The good faith of Oglethorpe in the offers of peace, his noble mein and sweetness of temper, conciliated the confidence of the red men, and he in turn was pleased with their simplicity, and sought for means to clear the glimmering ray of their minds, to guide their bewildered reason, and teach them to know the God whom they ignorantly adored.

For the welfare of Georgia he had renounced ease and the enjoyment of fortune to scorn danger and fare "much harder than any of the people who were settled there. He was merciful to the prisoner; a father to the emigrant; honestly zealous for the conversion of the Indians; invoking for the negro the panoply of the gospel. His heart throbbed warmly for all around him; he loved to relieve the indigent, to soothe the mourner; and his name became known as another expression for "vast benevolence of soul."

A TOUCHING SCENE.

We need not seek among the select classes to discover the finest poetry of sympathy. Recently a gamin, who seemed to have no friends in the world, was run over by a vehicle on Gratiot Avenue, Detroit, and fatally injured. After he had been in the hospital for a week, a boy about his own age and size, and looking as friendless and forlorn, called to ask about him and leave an orange. He seemed much embarrassed and would answer no questions. After that he came daily, always bringing something, if no more than an apple. A week later, when the nurse told him that Billy had no chance to get well, the strange boy waited around longer than usual, and finally asked if he could go in. He had been invited to many times before, but had always refused. Billy, pale and weak, and emaciated, opened his eyes in wonder at sight of the boy, and before he realized who it was the stranger bent close to his face and said, with moistened eyes: "Billy, can you forgive a feller? We was allus fighting, and I was allus too much for ye, but I am sorry! 'Fore ye die won't ye tell me ye haven't any grudge agin me?" The young lad, then almost in the shadow of death, reached up his thin, white arms, clasped them around the other's neck, and replied: "Don't cry, Bob—don't feel bad! I was ugly and mean, and I was heaving a stone at ye when the wagon hit me. If ye'll forgive me, I'll forgive you, and I'll pray for both o' us." Bob was half an hour late the morning Billy died; when the nurse took him to the shrouded corpse, he kissed the pale face tenderly, and gasped: "D—did he say anything about—about me?" "He spoke of you just before he died—asked if you were here," replied the nurse. "And may I go—go to the funeral?" "You may." And he did. He was the only mourner. His heart was the only one that ached. No tears were shed by others, and they left him sitting by the new-made grave with heart so big that he could not speak. If, under the crust of vice and ignorance, there are such springs of pure nobility, who shall grow weary of doing good?

A HEROINE.

If the average young lady is supposed to be luxurious and selfish, perhaps it is because she has never been put under trial in an emergency. At any rate, Lizzie McPherson entitled herself to a better verdict. A young lady acted the part of a heroine on Kearney Street, San Francisco, one evening, and what she did was all the more beautiful and brave because it was characterized by great presence of mind as well as extraordinary courage. The street was crowded with vehicles, and a woman and a child stood waiting at one of the crossings for an opportunity to walk over. Suddenly the child made a dart across the street and fell in front of a passing wagon. The young lady saw the dangerous position of the little one, and acting on that impulse that is of more service at times than the reasoning power, bounded to the rescue. The wagon-wheel was on the point of grazing the child's head. To have stopped to lift the little one would have been to lose the moment there was left to save its life. So she unhesitatingly put her foot in front of the wheel, and with her hands held on to the spokes until the wagon was stopped. The child was picked up unhurt, but her savior had her foot crushed, and from pain and excitement combined, fainted away when her deed of bravery was done. She was carried to a house in the neighborhood, and a physician attended to her injuries. When she recovered consciousness she was told by her brother that she had done that which might make her lame for life. Her answer was: "Don't scold. If I had hesitated a moment the child would have been crushed to death. The wheel would have passed over its head, and its only my foot that is hurt."

POCAHONTAS.

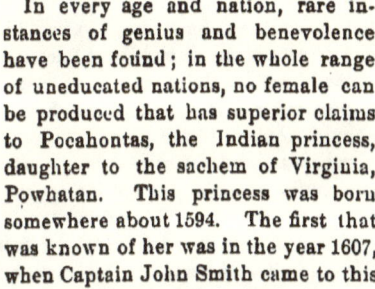

In every age and nation, rare instances of genius and benevolence have been found; in the whole range of uneducated nations, no female can be produced that has superior claims to Pocahontas, the Indian princess, daughter to the sachem of Virginia, Powhatan. This princess was born somewhere about 1594. The first that was known of her was in the year 1607, when Captain John Smith came to this continent for adventures, and in exploring the country about James River, was taken prisoner by some of the warriors of the tribes under Powhatan. The prowess he had shown when taken was sufficient for their justification in taking him off, for he had been a wonder and terror to all his foes. A council was called, the stories of the white man's prowess told, and Smith made up his mind to die. Pocahontas was an interested listener in the council. Heroism and beauty have always an effect on the female heart. The gentle feelings of humanity are the same in every race, and in every period of life they bloom, though unconsciously, even in the bosom of a child.

The manner of death decided upon for Smith was to be by beating him on the head with clubs while he was in a recumbent position, with a stone for a pillow. He was first bound, and then thrown down, and the clubs were uplifted, when Pocahontas, then a mere child, whose confiding fondness he had easily won, rushed forward and threw herself on the body of Smith, and protected his life at the risk of her own.

> " The war club poises for its fatal blow,
> The death mist swims before his darkened sight ;
> Forth springs the child, in tearful pity bold,
> Her head on his reclines, her arms his neck enfolds."

The impulse of mercy awakened within her breast, she clung firmly to his neck as his head was bowed to receive the strokes of the tomahawk. The barbarians, whose decision had long been held ·in suspense by the mysterious awe which Smith had inspired, now resolved to receive him as a friend, and to make him a partner of their councils. They tempted him to join their bands and lend assistance in an attack upon the white men at Jamestown, and when his decision of character succeeded in changing the current of their thoughts, they dismissed him with mutual promises of friendship and benevolence.

Some time after this, the savages becoming alarmed by witnessing Smith's wonderful feats, laid a plan to get him into their power under the pretense of wishing an interview with him in their territory. But Pocahontas, knowing the designs of the warriors, left the wigwam, after her father had gone to sleep, and ran more than nine miles through the woods to inform her friend, Captain Smith, of the danger that awaited him, either by stratagem or attack. At the age of seventeen or eighteen, Pocahontas married a pious young English officer named Thomas Rolfe, and went with him to England, where she was baptized and called Rebecca, and where she soon died. "It is not meet that such names should moulder in the grave." It was a barbarous life in which the little Pocahontas was bred. Her people always washed their young babies in the river on the coldest mornings to harden them. She was accustomed to see her old father sitting at the door of his cabin regarding with grim pleasure a string of his enemy's scalps suspended from tree to tree, and waving in the breeze. Such as her life made her she was—in her manners an untrained savage. But she was also the steadfast friend and helper of the feeble colony, and that is why her life is so full of interest to us.

A YOUNG HERO.

At the disaster which, not long since, destroyed the lives of many miners in the West Pittston mine, an incident occurred in which the heroic and pathetic are mingled. A boy of twelve years, named Martin Craghran, stood with a young companion on the carriage, waiting to be hoisted up from the mine out of impending danger, when it. flashed upon his mind that a number of workmen had not been warned of the terrible peril they were in. With a noble impulse of self-forgetful kindness, he resolved to rescue them if possible, and asked the other boy to go with him. This boy refused, and was safely drawn up—the last who was brought up unscathed. Martin rushed through the chambers and galleries of the mine alone, to carry the startling news to the imperiled miners. Then he hurried back to the shaft again, hoping to escape with his life. He waited for the carriage to descend, but the wire rope had melted, and the fire was now burning so fiercely above him that all hope of escape in that way (the only outlet) was cut off. He fled back to the miners again; but experience had taught them the utter hopelessness of escape by the ordinary way, and they had built a barricade in Martin's absence, which afforded them a temporary protection from the noxious gases and smoke that were slowly filling the mine. The barrier was solidly built, for upon the defense it afforded them against the smoke and gas depended the only chance that they had to live until the burning shaft was extinguished. Martin stood at the barrier and begged piteously to be admitted. The few survivors who heard him say the little fellow cried. But to have made a passage-way for him would have been death to all. So they were obliged to refuse him. After a little he went quietly away to the stable. He had been promoted to the position of mule-driver only the day before; and now he went to his mule, and there wrote with chalk upon a piece of board the names of those who were dear to him, and then lay down beside his mule to die. His body was found close to that of the poor animal, which, in its death agony, had rolled upon him and wounded his breast with a portion of the harness. So died this little hero in the dark.

CATHARINE BROWN.

It was a romantic country where this half-blooded Cherokee, for such was Catharine Brown, first drew her breath, and she seems to have acquired a natural taste for fine scenery. In 1816 the American Board of Foreign Missions sent Rev. Cyrus Kingsbury to the Cherokee nation for permission to establish a school in their territory. This was granted, and a school opened at Chickamaúga, within the territory of Tennessee. Catharine having heard of this school, although a hundred miles away, attended the same, where she soon learned to speak and read English words of one syllable. She was modest, gentle and virtuous, with a sweet and affectionate disposition. She was the most docile of all the missionary pupils, and her future progress was wonderfully rapid. In three months she had learned to read and write acceptably. This exceeds the progress of any one on record, in this or any other country. Having been baptized, in June, 1820, she undertook to teach a school at Creekpath, near her father's house. She showed the greatest zeal in the cause of enlightening her countrywomen, for those of all ages came to learn something of her. She established religious exercises in her father's house, and brought many to Christianity. She was not contented with the measure of information she had acquired, but intended to push her studies into higher branches of knowledge which she knew to exist, but while she contemplated these great things for herself and nation her health began to decline. The change from flying through the groves and paddling the canoe to such a sedentary life, which she must have led in acquiring so much knowledge in so short a time, would have naturally undermined the strongest constitution. In her sickness she discovered the greatest resignation and the most exalted piety. She had made a deep impression on her people, and they watched the progress of her disease with the most poignant anxiety. She died in 1823, aged twenty-three, and would have been, in the early ages of Christianity, ranked with saints and martyrs, and at this time deserves to be held in sweet remembrance. Catharine Brown must be ranked with Pocahontas, the loveliest daughter of the wilderness; both forming the highest proof that the children of the forest have talents, and strong and noble affections, and only require instruction to rival those of the Anglo-Saxon blood. When we discover such talents and virtues in the aborigines, the philanthropist, as well as the Christian, mourns to think that this race of beings will soon disappear in our country, but we must console ourselves that the hand of God is in this.

A PLUCKY CAPTAIN.

The great plains of the West are occasionally visited during the winter with a "norther." Exposure to its full force is death to man or beast. The icy wind cuts like a knife. No clothing or fur coat prevents it from penetrating to the body and extracting every particle of dry heat. Animals, even the thickly covered buffalo, fly before a "norther," and seek the protection of a wooded ravine. Many hunters and plainsmen, caught by these storms where there is no shelter of thicket or ravine, are frozen to death every winter. Once a company of the

Second Cavalry was caught in a "norther." Nothing but the pluck of the captain saved the men from freezing to death. There was no friendly ravine or thicket in which to camp. Their salvation was to keep moving. For thirty miles they marched in the teeth of a terrific gale and blinding snow storm. Each man, in turn, was made to lead his horse and open the way through the snow. Some of the men threw themselves into the snow and declared they would die rather than take another step. Orders, entreaties and threats availed not. Lie on the snow and die they would, until the captain, belaboring them with the flat of his sabre, beat them into making an effort to march. The plucky officer brought every man safely into the fort.

THOMAS NELSON, JR.

Self-sacrificing patriotism was frequently exhibited during the Revolutionary struggle, and oftentimes private property was cheerfully given for the public good. Everywhere personal ease and family endearments were abandoned for the hardships of public life. Thomas Nelson, jr., of Yorktown, Virginia, was of that class of patriots. He was educated in England, and upon returning home watched the progress of difficulties between Great Britain and her colonies with lively interest. He first appeared in public life in 1774, when he was elected a member of the house of burgesses, of Virginia, and he was one of eighty-one members of that assembly who, when dissolved by the royal governor (Dunmore,) met at the Raleigh tavern, organized, and appointed delegates to the first continental congress. He was actively engaged in the drama of the times; proposed organizing a militia for defense, was elected governor, sent to congress, and was a powerful auxiliary in the siege of Yorktown in the autumn of 1781. During that siege his own fine mansion, situated within the enemy's lines, was occupied by British officers. He observed that in the storm of balls which the besiegers were pouring upon the town and the British works, his own house was spared. He begged the cannoniers not to regard his property with favor, and actually directed a piece himself so that the balls would fall upon the mansion. It had the effect to drive the officers from that strong retreat, and no doubt hastened the surrender of Cornwallis. A month after the surrender General Nelson heeded the warnings of declining health and retired to private life. The remainder of his days were spent in quiet, alternately at his mansion in Yorktown and upon his estate at Offley. He died at the former place on the 4th of January, 1789, in the fifty-third year of his age.

DAVID BRAINARD.

To leave the endearments of home and the pleasures of civilized life, and spend the strength of manhood among pagans, with the sole aim of doing good to the needy, is true heroism—an exhibition of chivalry worthy of the honors of knighthood. Prominent on the list of such self-sacrificing champions is the name of David Brainard, eminent as a missionary among the Indians of our land. He entered Yale College in 1739, but was expelled for a very trivial offense. In 1743 he began his famous labors among the Indians. He lived in a wigwam, slept on straw, and ate boiled corn, hasty-pudding and samp. Though feeble in body, and often ill, he persevered; and when, in 1744, his flock agreed to go to Stockbridge, he went with his glad tidings to his Delaware Indians. Among the New Jersey Indians at Crosswicks, he was remarkably successful. In less than a year he baptized seventy-seven converts, and the whole tribe became thoroughly reformed in their morals. His health gradually gave way, and he was compelled to leave the field of duty, where his heart lingered. He became engaged in marriage to a daughter of Jonathan Edwards, in which family he took up his abode, and when his flower of life faded, and when the leaves began to fall in autumn, he fell like an apple early ripe, into the lap of the grave. He was but twenty-nine years of age when he died, in 1747.

THOMAS JEFFERSON.

This honored American might well have said with Horace of old, "I have erected a monument more lasting than brass, which neither the winds nor the rains can destroy." For beside the perishable monuments that to-day keep green his memory, the famous instrument of the Declaration of Independence, of which he was the author, stands as an imperishable one. While yet a student, in 1765, he heard Patrick Henry's famous speech against the stamp act, and it lighted a flame of patriotism in young Jefferson's soul that burned brighter and brighter until the hour of fearless action arrived. He was a member of the Virginia Assembly and of the continental congress. He was an excellent writer, and for this reason, among others, he was appointed to draft the Declaration of Independence. From the fullness of his own mind, without consulting one single book, Jefferson drafted the Declaration. He submitted it separately to Franklin and John Adams, accepting from each of them one or two verbal corrections, and then submitted it to congress. The Declaration was not signed by the members of congress on the day on which it was agreed to, but it was duly authenticated by the president and secretary and published to the world. The nation, when it made the choice of a day for its great anniversary, selected not the day of the resolution of independence, when it closed the past, but that of the declaration of principles on which it opened its new career.

From about the beginning of 1779, when he was governor of Virginia, having succeeded Patrick Henry, until the close of 1780, the British and German troops captured at Saratoga were quartered in his vicinity, and he greatly endeared himself to them by his uniform kindness. It was a most trying time for Virginia, and Jefferson, sagaciously perceiving that a military man was needed in the executive office, declined a re-election and was succeeded by General Nelson, of Yorktown. After holding various public and diplomatic positions, in 1796 he was chosen Vice President of the United States, and in the spring of 1801 he took his seat as chief magistrate of the nation. With untiring perseverance he succeeded in establishing that yet flourishing institution, the University of Virginia, and until the last his life was spent in pursuits of public utility. The latter years of his life were clouded with pecuniary embarrassments. He sold his library to the federal government in 1815, consisting of six thousand volumes. He survived that great sacrifice eleven years, and then his spirit took its flight, while his countrymen were celebrating the fiftieth anniversary of the independence of the United States. It was a beautiful trait in his character that he was free from envy. A strange and striking coincidence closed the life of this great man and John Adams. Both expired on the same day, and at almost the same hour. They were both on the committee that framed the Declaration of Independence, both voted for that instrument just fifty years before; both signed it; both had been foreign ministers, and both had been presidents of the Republic they had helped to establish. Proud patriots they, and the nation still reveres their memory. In the words of Webster, their great eulogist, "Their name liveth evermore!"

MARGARET PRIOR.

The noble, self-sacrificing spirit of this woman will ever be commended. She was the mother of seven children, all but one dying during infancy. Subsequently her husband was lost at sea. In 1814 she again married and moved to New York. Her husband, Wm. Prior, was a benevolent and public spirited man. We first find her in the more conspicuous "walks of usefulness" in 1818 and 1819. She made arrangements with a kind neighbor to furnish soup to the destitute three times a week, and then began her work among the lowly. In this way it is believed that many were relieved from starvation. Notwithstanding her arduous public duties, she managed her household affairs with care, neatness and regularity. The time that some spend in fashionable and heartless calls she spent in industry and humanity. By rising early, working late, observing the strictest rules of economy, and subjecting herself, at times, to self-denials, she was able to visit the suffering. Passing through the suburbs of the city one day, her attention was arrested by the chime of youthful voices. Seeing that the music proceeded from some little beggar girls, who were sitting in the sun beside the fence and singing a Sunday school hymn, she inquired of them what they were doing, when the following dialogue occurred: "We were cold, ma'am, and are getting warm in the sun." "Where do you live?" "In Twentieth street, ma'am." "Why have you come so far away from your home?" "To get some food and some things to make a fire." "Why were you singing?" "To praise God; we go to the Sunday school, and our teacher says if we are good children God will never let us want." Pleased with the modest and artless answers to her questions, the good woman took them across the street, procured each of them a loaf of bread, gave them some pious counsel and left them with smiles on their faces and gratitude in their hearts. Such were the doings, such was the character of Margaret Prior. We see her organizing week-day and Sabbath-schools, industrial associations, and temperance societies, establishing soup houses, and orphan asylums; visiting the sick, the poor, the idle, the culprit, the outcast; pointing the dying to a risen Savior, leading the destitute by the hand to the place of relief, the idle to houses of industry, and warning the outlaw and the corrupt of the certain and terrible doom that would attend persistency in their downward course. With the sweetness, gentleness, simplicity and delicacy, so becoming in women under all circumstances, were blended in her character energy that was unconquerable, courage that danger could not flinch, and firmness that human power could not bend.

JAMES MADISON.

In these times of political intrigue, when politicians for the most part, gain their ascendancy through bribes, a character pure and spotless, like that of James Madison, who could be an honest politician and yet gain power, presents itself as a model to the young men of to-day. He received a good education and early was attracted by political affairs. In 1777, after he had been a member of the State Legislature of Virginia, and other executive bodies, he lost the suffrages of his constituents because it was alleged that he would not "treat" the people to liquor and could not make a speech! Mr. Madison was again a member of the Virginia Assembly from 1784 to 1786, where he was the champion of every wise and liberal policy, especially in religious matters. After serving eight years as Chief Magistrate of the Republic, Mr. Madison, in March, 1817, retired to his paternal estate of Montpelier, where he remained in retirement until his death, which occurred almost twenty years afterward. He had married an accomplished widow, in Philadelphia, and with her, his books, friends, and in agricultural pursuits, he passed the evening of his days in great happiness.

A TOUCHING ACT.

Opportunities are few and seldom on a battle-field for parting tears or touches of tenderness. And yet scenes of carnage and fiercest human strife and passion have sometimes been lit by the sweetest gleams of piety, and Christian loving-kindness has appeared strangely hand in hand with the fierceness which takes the sword. One of the severest battles of the late civil war was that at Mt. Crawford, near Staunton, Va., June 5, 1864, generally known as the battle of Piedmont. It resulted disastrously to the Southern cause, and fifteen hundred of the Confederates were taken prisoners, beside the loss in killed and wounded left upon the field. Passing over the ground in the path of the fight, a Union surgeon found among the wounded a boy fourteen years old, who had been shot through the stomach. He begged for water, and when the surgeon had given him a drink from his canteen and examined his wound, he said, " Can I get well again ?" The surgeon shook his head. The poor lad turned very pale, closed his eyes, a few tears trickled from the lids, and he seemed to be praying. He had been forced to join the army, he said, when he did not want to leave home, and now he could never see his mother and sister again. What would they do? A young Federal officer riding near the spot while the boy was drinking from the surgeon's canteen, had stopped his horse, deeply affected by the sight and sufferings of one so young. The sadness of the little soldier when he first knew that he must die went to the young man's heart. He sprang from his horse, took the sufferer's hands in his own, and leaning his face lovingly against the face of the lad, soothed him as if he had been a babe, and then offered a prayer, that in beauty and yearning tenderness was like the prayer of a mother. Rising, the young officer laid a caressing hand on the poor boy's head, murmured a " God bless you !" and hastened away where duty called him. The minutes of the little soldier's life were numbered, and he soon closed his eyes forever; but the gentle, Christian deed of one whom the fearful code of war called his enemy, had softened his hard bed of death. This young officer was Captain Meigs, afterward Major Meigs, who was killed near Harrisonburg, Va. One loves to think that he and the sad young soul he once comforted have sought and found each other in the world where none who have prayed together on earth can ever again wear the uniform of mutual foes.

MRS. FANNY RICKETTS.

No page in the history of the late bloody war is so brilliant as that illuminated by a record of the noble sacrifices and exploits of heroic woman. Among this bright galaxy of noble women, the one whose name heads this sketch was foremost in her unwavering and heroic devotion. In January, 1856, Miss Lawrence was married to James B. Ricketts, then a captain in the First Artillery, U. S. A., and immediately went with him to the distant south-western frontier of the Republic, on the Rio Grande, where his company was stationed. When in camp, Mrs. Ricketts greatly endeared herself to the men of her husband's company by constant acts of kindness to the sick, and by manifesting a cheerful spirit away from the comforts and refinements of American civilization. At the commencement of the war her husband's company was ordered back. Here military rules separated her from her husband, and from Washington she could only watch and pray, listening with heavy heart to the far-off roar. On the evening of July 21, 1861, the dreadful news of her husband's terrible wounds and then his death, were announced to her. The agonized wife was plunged into an abyss of despair. Learning afterward that her husband was not dead, as yet, but still lingering, she procured permission to visit him, then a prisoner in the south. Proceeding as far as the enemy's pickets, she was stopped and delayed some time. Upon being required to sign a patrol that she would not act as a spy, and notwithstanding her extreme anxiety to avoid detention, she indignantly tore the paper into pieces before the officer's eyes, replying, "I am no spy, but the wife of a wounded officer, and will go as your prisoner, but never sign a patrol." Demanding a guide and passport she proceeded to the headquarters of General Joseph E. Johnston, and was directed to a house in the still blood-stained field of carnage, where her husband had been carried. In the court-yard of the house lay rows of the wounded and dead. Under the window she glanced at a fearful pile of human limbs, the accumulation of two day's amputation. Passing up stairs, amid the most harrowing and blood-curdling scenes, she found six wounded men in a small chamber, five ranged along the wall on the floor, and one, more pallid than the rest, very still, on a bloody stretcher. This was her husband! At first he was unconscious, but at length feebly murmured in her ear, "I knew you would come!" Though her husband's life was hanging as by a thread, so that a little neglect might be fatal to him, all night long she could not resist the appeals that were heard all about her for water. She rose from the floor beside her husband, and taking part of the small supply that a surgeon had brought for his hot and swollen leg from a spring half a mile distant, she groped her way among the groaning and prostrate forms, moistening their parched lips. For two weeks Mrs. Ricketts remained with her husband in the house where she found him. The stench of the battle-field becoming so great, the camp was abandoned, and the prisoners removed to Richmond, where the situation, if possible, was worse. Several times did the devoted wife plead against amputating her wounded husband's leg. Much of the time he lay unconscious, and for weeks his life depended entirely on the untiring patience and skill with which his wife soothed down the rudeness of his prison house, cheering him and other prisoners who were so fortunate as to be in the room with him, and alleviating the slow misery that was settling like a pall upon them. Like a death sentence finally came the order that Captain Ricketts had been selected as one of the thirteen high officials who would be transferred to other quarters to be killed at any moment the news should be received that a similar number of Confederate officers held in custody in the north were killed. With the dawn of the next morning, brave Mrs. Ricketts addressed a letter to Mrs. Cooper, and thus the secretary who had issued the fearful order including Captain Ricketts, was moved and issued a subsequent order, that "all the wounded officers had been exempted as hostages." Mrs. Ricketts' health was being undermined, and when the close of the year came they were permitted to leave Libby prison. Her husband was made brigadier-general. The battle of Antietam called her again to his side, as he was wounded in the same leg as in the former battle, by his horse being shot and rolling upon him. During all the summer and fall of the year in which the battle of Gettysburg was fought, she continued her labors among those who seemed most to require her attentions, her husband's health being recovered and he having returned to participate in all the battles in which his corps was engaged. At the battle of Cedar Run, General Ricketts received his third serious wound, which came nearer being fatal than any former injury. For four anxious and weary months she was hanging over his couch, and doing everything that love and skill could suggest to save a life that had now become doubly precious to her for the sufferings and the anxieties which had been devolved upon both by the stern demands of the country. With the first boom of the deadly thunder at Manassas she had been called away from her life of joyous ease and peaceful love, and so long as the noise of that long war lasted she had known no rest nor intermission in her labors of womanly care and devotion.

PATRICK HENRY.

"Ceasar had his Brutus, Charles First his Cromwell and George Third "— "Treason, Treason!"

"If this be treason, make the most of it!" So exclaimed Patrick Henry in the Virginia Assembly when the obnoxious laws of taxation, coupled with an imparative order to house and feed the British, was announced. Henry was the son of a Virginia planter, and was born on the 29th of May, 1736. He was not an ardent student, and his early years gave promise of a useless life. He married at eighteen, and passed most of his time in idleness at the tavern of his father-in-law, where he often served customers at the bar. Having utterly failed in farming and in trade, he made an attempt at the law, and after only a month and a half's study, had the boldness to ask for license to practice. This was granted on the condition that he should extend his studies before undertaking to practice. His first effort was the celebrated Parsons case, which was a contest betwen the clergy and the state legislature, on the question of an annual stipend claimed by the former. Henry's eloquence, after a rambling introduction, electrified judge, jury, and people. The jury brought in a verdict of one penny damages, and the people took Henry upon their shoulders, and carried him in triumph about the court-house yard. Patrick Henry knew not fear; nor did his success conquer his aversion to the black letter of the law books. He loved to stroll through the forests, hunting deer for days together, taking his only rest under the trees; and as he wandered about with his ever-ready musket in his hand, his serene mind was ripening for duty, he knew not how, by silent communion with nature.

In 1769 he was admitted to the bar of the general court, and was recognized as a leader in legal and political matters until the Revolution broke out. He became the authoized leader of the people against the aristocracy. In the first continental congress, he was one of the delegates, and in that famous assembly he was hailed as the champion of constitutional liberty, and his wonderful eloquence was at once recognized. At the Richmond convention, of which Henry was the moving spirit, his resolutions to organize the militia and put the colony.

in an attitude of defense, met with great opposition. He replied in a burning speech, in which occur the memorable words: "There is no retreat but in submission and slavery. Our chains are already forged; their clanking may be heard in the plains of Boston; the next gale that sweeps from the north will bring the clash of resounding arms. I know not what course others may take; but, as for me, give me liberty or give me death!" Without an opposing voice the resolutions were adopted; and very soon afterward came the news of the battles at Lexington and Concord. Shortly afterward two regiments were raised, and Henry was appointed commander of all the forces to be raised. Washington nominated him for the office of secretary of state, in 1795, but Mr. Henry declined it. In 1799, he was only prevented from accepting a diplomatic position to France by feeble health and advanced age. A few weeks afterward his disease became alarmingly active, and he expired at his seat, at Red Hill, in Charlotte County, June 6, 1799, at the age of almost sixty-three years.

HUMANITY REWARDED.

Among the early settlements of New Hampshire were several on the Piscataqua river, in the neighborhood of the present town of Dover. For a while the aborigines and the whites were [on amicable terms, and the former not unfrequently paid the latter a friendly visit. On one of those occasions, a pappoose was suddenly seized with illness, and its mother was obliged to remain several days. She found shelter and accommodations with a widow, who received her cordially, and nursed the feeble infant as her own. Such kindness would not be forgotten, even by savages; and when, after the lapse of years, the bow was bent and the hatchet raised against the settlement where the widow resided, the Indians placed a strong guard around her house; and, although the butchering was terrible, she and her family were unharmed.

PHOEBE PHILLIPS.

This remarkable woman, who died at Andover, in the year 1818, was born at Cambridge, Massachusetts. She was the daughter of Mr. Foxcroft, a gentleman of wealth and high standing, who gave her a good education. To her intimate acquaintance with the faculty of Harvard University from childhood, may, in some measure, be attributed her elegant style of conversation, which surpassed that of any one, male or female, in this country. She saw the subject under consideration in all its bearings, and clothed it in most felicitous language. There was no redundancy, no stint, no singularity—except that of supreme refinement—nothing to excite surprise in her conversation; but the most learned listened with profound admiration at her taste and skill in language. She was fond of her pen, and took delight in keeping up an extensive correspondence with literary and religious persons. She wrote with great ease and rapidity, in chirography at once plain as a printed page, and whose beauty was only exceeded by the thought it contained. She was married to Samuel Phillips, of Andover;

a young man at that period most zealously engaged in the cause of his country, anxious for its political prosperity, and for its advancement in learning; and he found a most admirable coadjutor in his wife. During the dark period of the Revolution, he sat up until midnight with the females of the household making garments for the poor destitute soldiers, and in scraping lint or cutting bandages for the hospitals. The sick in her neighborhood, of all classes, were inquired after, and everything that could administer to their comfort was sent from her hospitable mansion. The academy founded by her husband and his uncle was in the immediate vicinity of her residence, and every pupil's health was a subject of her attention. Devoted to religion with more "than the cloistered maiden's zeal;" she had not a particle of bigotry in her disposition, and one might have lived with her for years without knowing her sentiment upon any particular point in divinity. At her table—for her husband was so deeply engaged in politics and business, that he left all of the household cares upon her—might be found almost every day in the week, clergymen who met nowhere else—from a difference in creeds—and persons of distinction in the various callings of life, and from different parts of the country. For more than forty years this hospitality was uninterrupted, and her cares unceasing.

Her person was striking, tall above most women; her mein was majestic, without any awkwardness from her height; her features were prominent, but softened by a fine, mild expression; and her large, blue eyes were full of sweetness of temper, while they beamed with genius. There has scarcely been a single individual who ever knew her that had not some rememberance of her talents and virtues in his mind, and most of them could relate some acts of kindness toward themselves. She made no parade of attainments, but all her information seemed to flow in conversation, as though it were intuitive, and addressed to those in company as if she considered every one about her superior to herself in memory and reasoning powers; in fact, in every attainment and gift. When others judged by a lesson, or a few recitations, she formed her opinion from some act or remark of the boy, which might have passed unnoticed by others. With all her firmness of soul, she had a heart most feelingly alive to the misfortunes of others. Often "her pity gave ere charity began;" and she was distressed even at the sufferings of the wicked. A lad seeing from her window a wretched looking man going to the whipping-post to receive corporal punishment for a petty larceny—sentenced by the justice of the peace to this ignominy—strove to conceal a tear, but this excellent woman observed it. With one starting in her own eye, she said to him, "When you become a law-maker examine the subject of corporal punishment, and see if it is not unnatural, vindictive, and productive of much evil." In early manhood he became a legislator, and remembering the words which made a strong impression at that time, he called the attention of the assembly to the subject, and in the course of a short time had the satisfacton of announcing to her that the statute book had been expurgated in this respect, and that there was, in future, to be no more corporal punishment for any offense less than capital. After her husband's death she was one of the founders of the theological seminary at Andover, and took a deep interest in the institution as long as she lived.

JANET McCREA.

The fate of this young woman has excited the sympathies of the whole people of the United States. She was the daughter of James McCrea, a clergyman of New Jersey, who died before the Revolution. After her father's death Janet resided with her brother, at Albany, who removed to the neighborhood of Fort Edward. She was a young lady of twenty-three years of age, amiable, and well educated. She was related to one of the American officers at Fort Edward, but, on the alarm given by the retreat of the American army from the lakes, she had left her home for a safe retreat in Fort Miller; but when the American forces thought it prudent to retire from that fortress to Vermont, see did not think proper to go

with them, and returned to Sandy Hill, the place of her usual residence. Rumor after rumor soon reached her here of the approach of the Indians, and she knew not whither to fly. The whole country from the lakes was in great consternation, and she set out for Fort Edward with some other females. Her fears were increased, for she felt no confidence in either side. She was on American ground, but was betrothed to an American who had taken sides with the British, and had gone to Canada, where he was made captain of a company. The lovers had managed to keep up a correspondence, and he was informed when he reached Fort Anne, that his inamorata was concealed in a house a few miles from Sandy Hill. To go there himself would be dangerous to both, as the woods were infested with scouting parties of American troups, and he, as a Tory, would have been harshly dealt with if taken by them; but, to make all sure, he engaged a party of confidential Indians to take his horse and go to her place of concealment, and bring her to him in safety. The party reached the place and she received the letter. He urged her in his letter not to hesitate a moment in putting herself under their protection, but she had some sad misgivings. The Indians had been a terror to that part of the country, and the tales she had heard in her childhood came quickly upon her distracted mind; but the voice of a lover is law to a confiding woman. She put herself under their guidance, and they had proceeded on their journey, she on horseback and they on foot, to near a small spring which may now be seen, when a dispute arose as to who should receive the reward, or how it would be shared. A quarrel ensued, in which one of them killed her by striking her with a tomahawk. Occasion was thereby given to inflame the populace and to blacken the royal cause. The cruelties of the Indians and the cause in which they were engaged were associated together, and presented in one view to the alarmed inhabitants. This massacre was probably no more horrible than many others; but it was susceptible of embellishment, and everywhere produced a deep impression. Many patriots were led to join the army, and many royalists to desert a cause which permitted such atrocities. Some one of the Indians, with their usual regard to truth, made her lover acquainted with the facts, and another proved his assertions by exhibiting the scalp. He knew the long golden tresses of Miss McCrea, and in defiance of all danger flew to the spot to realize the horrid tale. He tore away the thinly spread leaves and earth, clasped the still bleeding body in his arms, and wrapping it in his cloak bore it to the first wagon he could find, and there hid it from the sight of the world until he could dispose of it according to his affections. The driver was bribed to silence. The lover sat by the wagon all night in a state but little short of a quiet delirium, now and then arousing himself to a furious determination to immolate the first Indian he could find; but they were all in their lairs. The morning sun arose, and the wagon went on, he having determined to take the corpse on with him to some spot hallowed by the graves of others, and there deposit the sacred relic of the beloved of his soul. But his neglect of duty and strange demeanor, caused him to be watched by his superior officers, who heard something of the rumor, and they discovered the secret that the corpse of Miss McCrea was in the wagon. They instantly ordered the wagon to stop, and the corpse to be buried by the wayside; kindly allowing Captain Jones to stay a few moments, "to see her decent limbs composed," and laid in the bosom of the earth, a coffin having been procured. The grave is about four miles from Fort Edward. Captain Jones, it is said, survived her but a few years; and this melancholy event is supposed to have brought him to the grave. Perhaps the tragical death of this amiable girl has given a degree of romance to her virtues and personal charms; but it is agreed by all who knew her, that she was amiable, virtuous, and accomplished. The tomahawk and the scalping knife have nearly become extinct as weapons of dread to the women and children of our favored country. To our primitive mothers they were something more than "air drawn daggers," creatures of the imagination; for on their blade and gudgeon were often real gouts of blood.

ELI WHITNEY.

Beyond all doubt or question, the invention of the cotton-gin, just at the close of the eighteenth century, was an event which most wonderfully accelerated the high career of the United States in an industrial point of view; and indeed, revolutionized, by an extraordinary impetus, the manufactures and commerce of the world. It may be regarded, in a word, as the first key which was applied to the unlocking of those wondrous natural capabilities of the new born republic, the continued development of which has given her such a foremost place in respect to material and political power among the nations of the earth. Every labor-saving machine is a gain to humanity; and every inventor of such machines is a public benefactor. High on the list of such worthies is the name of Eli Whitney, the inventor of the cotton-gin. At an early age he gave indications of that mechanical and inventive talent for which he was afterward so greatly celebrated. Having entered the college at New Haven at the age of twenty-three, he graduated afterward with high honors. Going to Georgia, accompanying the widow of General Greene, he was disappointed in securing the position of tutor that he had desired. Upon the invitation of Mrs. Greene, he made her home his residence. During an afternoon social gathering at the lady's house, his genius was aroused to its utmost accomplishments, upon the remark being made that the cotton and agricultural interests of Georgia were greatly depressed. The great trouble existed in the fact that there was no means of cleansing the green seed-cotton, or separating it from its seed. In response to suggestions made, Mrs. Greene, who knew of Whitney's ingenious turn of mind in the sphere of mechanics, naively remarked: "Well, gentlemen, apply to my young friend, Mr. Whitney. He can make anything;" and suiting the action to the word, she led them into the room where her tambour was kept, and exhibited it among other things as evidences of Whitney's singular skill. In a few months he had advanced so far and so successfully with his machine as to leave no doubt of his having achieved a complete triumph. The report of the invention spread very rapidly throughout the South, exciting intense interest. The machine was examined with delight, for it would do the work of months in a single day. With it one man could do the work of a thousand. It opened a way to immense wealth to the southern planters. Whitney finally went to his native state, patented his invention, and, in partnership with Mr. Miller, commenced the manufacture of machines for Georgia. Many infringement suits arose, his shop burned, and all its contents together with his papers. He became bankrupt; and the inventor of the cotton-gin, which has been worth hundreds of millions of dollars to the people of the South, never received sufficient income to pay his actual outlays and losses. He was treated unfairly by juries, especially everywhere among those who profited by his invention. Even Congress denied his application to extend his patent. Disappointed and disgusted with the injustice of his fellow men, Mr. Whitney turned his attention to other pursuits. For a time he manufactured fire-arms for the United States. He was successful in this departure as he also was in the choice of his excellent wife. He ultimately acquired a fortune—a strange but most deserved sequel to his hitherto checkered career. The progress and value of the cotton production in the United States, under the impetus given to it by Whitney's invention, may be characterized as simply prodigious; and, in the mind of the philosophic statesman and student, the story of the cotton-gin will forever weave itself, most intimately and wonderfully, with those great themes and events which make up the nation's history. After great suffering from disease, Whitney died near New Haven, on the 8th of January, 1825, at the age of fifty-nine years.

_____

MRS. E. E. GEORGE.

When our present subject conceived the noble purpose of consecrating herself to her country, and applied for admission to the sanitary commission, her age seemed against her, for she had reached that period in life which suggests the quiet of the fireside and the comforts of home, rather than a rude, changeful, and wearing succession of exhausting toils and midnight vigils.

"True," she said, "I am old; but my health is good, and I am very desirous to do something for those who are every day exposing their lives for our country."

She made frequent trips between Memphis and Corinth, with various hospital supplies and sanitary comforts for the men; and although the cars were often fired into by the guerrillas and squads of confederate cavalry, she acted as though fear of death, while in the line of duty, was a passion that had no place in her calm and well regulated mind. During the battle at Jonesboro, she was dressing the wounded in a tent so near the front as to be in range of the enemy's guns; a shell from one of their batteries pierced the tent, and, exploding within a few feet of where she was standing, killed two wounded men. When asked if the circumstance did not somewhat alarm her, she replied, "No, I was not alarmed, for I looked upon it as simply the intention of Providence to test my courage."

Her labors among the Indiana soldiers at Wilmington exhausted her, and here it was that this excellent lady finished her toils, and crowned her long and active career of beneficence by deliberate self-martyrdom. By day she was constantly occupied in superintending the manufacture of clothing for the naked; at night she went into the hospitals, and depriving herself of sleep passed many of the hours of darkness in nursing the greatest sufferers. For more than two years she had taken only brief periods of rest; she was advanced in years, and the peculiar form of typhoid fever which attacked the released prisoners for whom she so heroically labored, was in a high degree contagious. The death of this noble woman was sudden, while the preparations were in progress for taking her back to her home. Her martyrdom was prolific of great good, and she will long be remembered for her devotion.

_____

WILLIAM BARTON.

For his noble protest against imprisonment for debt will the name of William Barton be revered. He was a worthy scion of old Rhode Island stock, and was born in Providence in 1750. In the war for independence we find him among the most daring of those who gave the British great annoyance after they had taken possession of Rhode Island. When our subject was lieutenant-colonel of militia, General Prescott, an arrogant, tyrannical man, was the commander-in-chief of the enemy in that section, and the people suffered much at his hands. In trying to get rid of him all plans failed, until Colonel Barton's plan was successfully executed. On a sultry night in July, 1777, Barton, with a few trusty followers, crossed Narragansett Bay from Warwick Point, in whale-boats, directly through a British fleet, and landed in a sheltered cove a short distance from Prescott's headquarters. They proceeded stealthily in two divisions, and secured the sentinel and the outside door of the house; then Barton boldly entered, with four strong men and a negro, and proceeded to Prescott's room on the second floor; the door was locked on the inside; the negro stepping back a few paces used his head as a battering ram, and the door flew open. Prescott, supposing the intruders to be robbers, sprang from his bed and seized his gold watch; the next moment Barton's hand was laid on his shoulder, and he was admonished that he was a prisoner, and must be silent. Not allowing him to dress, the whole party returned, undiscovered by the sentinels of the fleet. Prescott's mouth was kept shut by a pistol at each ear. The prisoner first spoke after landing, and said, "Sir, you have made a bold push to-night." Barton cooly replied, "We have been fortunate." Congress presented their thanks and an elegant sword to Barton, and in December he was promoted to the rank and pay of colonel of the Continental army; a grant of land in Vermont was also given him. In after years the land in Vermont proved to be an unfortunate gift; by the transfer of some of it he became entangled in the meshes of the law, and was imprisoned for debt for many years in his old age. When LaFayette was in the country in 1825, he heard of the situation of his companion-in-arms, paid the debt and set him at liberty. It was a significant rebuke to the American people. This brave man died in Providence, in 1831, at the age of eighty-four years.

THE MOTHER OF PRESIDENT POLK.

President Polk's mother, who died at Columbia, Tennessee, in the winter of 1851-2, was a member of the Presbyterian church, a highly exemplary Christian, and a faithful mother. The lessons which she taught her son in youth were not forgotten when he arrived at manhood, and had risen to the highest office in the gift of a free and sovereign people. A single anecdote will show the abiding recollection and influence of her teachings.

A gentleman who once visited Mr. Polk at the White House, remarked to him that his respect for the Sabbath was highly gratifying to the religious sentiment of the country; whereupon he made the following reply: "I was taught by a pious mother to fear God, and keep his commandments, and I trust that no cares of a government of my own will ever tempt me to forget what I owe to the government of God."

AMOS OGDEN.

During the year 1771, the Pennymite and Yankee war was raging. In this Wyoming contest no braver man than Captain Ogden devoted himself to rendering the fortifications impregnable. In courage no way inferior to that of Ogden, the Connecticut Yankee party, in Captain Butler, had a commander skilled in the arts of war, and so thorough was the investment about Fort Wyoming, and so closely pressed, that not a man could venture out for fuel, food or water without being met by a volley. The garrison, containing nearly one hundred souls, soon felt the pressure of actual want and the dread of approaching famine. Husbanding his resources, however, in the most prudent manner, and in the darkness and stillness of night bringing up from the river sufficient water to last through the day, Ogden determined to hold out to the last extremity. But without aid, time must exhaust his provisions, and then to surrender would be inevitable. The descent of Captain Butler had been made with such secrecy and celerity that not the slightest notice of his approach had been received. To convey intelligence to headquarters opened the only avenue of hope, and Ogden, as the achievement demanded the utmost boldness, promptitude and wisdom, determined to be himself the messenger. The deed alone was sufficient to immortalize any man, and stamp his name with the title of hero. A little past midnight on the 12th of July, when all was quiet, one of the Yankee sentinels saw something floating on the river having a very suspicious appearance. A shot awakened attention and directed the eyes of every other sentinel to the spot. A volley was poured in, but produced no apparent effect; the thing still floating gently with the current the firing was suspended. Captain Ogden had tied his clothes in a bundle and fastened his hat to the top, to this was connected a string of several yards in length which he fastened to his arm. Letting himself noiselessly into the water, swimming on his back so deeply as only to allow his lips to breathe— the whole movement demanding the most extraordinary skill and self-possession —he floated down, drawing the bundle after him. As he had calculated, this being the only object apparent, drew the fire of his foes. He escaped unhurt, and when out of danger dressed himself in his drenched clothes, perforated with bullets, and with the speed of the roebuck, was, in three days, one hundred and twenty miles distant, over a most rough and inhospitable wilderness, where he apprised his friends of the state of affairs. The services of that man, we are sure, have never been justly appreciated, and we fear have not been fairly rewarded.

THOMAS WILLIAMS.

All the deeds of daring, manly heroism and noble defenses made during the Revolutionary struggle will never be known. To live, men and women alike not only were brave, but heroic in the highest sense of the term. The atrocities of the Indians were harrowing even to contemplate. The gallant defense of his father's house, by Sergeant Thomas Williams, deserves to be especially recorded. On the day the fort was attacked, a party of Indians made an assault on the house. The father, sick and confined to his bed, was unable to lend any assistance. Sergeant Williams, and a brother quite young, were the only persons capable of offering the least resistance. Twice the Indians rushed up to the door and attempted in vain to force an entrance. Several balls were fired into the house through openings in the logs, one of which severely wounded the sick father. All this was accompanied by horrid yells, as if demons had visited the upper air. Having lost a brother the preceding fall, and belonging himself to the army, Mr. Williams knew his fate depended on his coolness and courage. He must base all hope on these alone. He had two guns, one of which the lad loaded while he fired the other. Watching his time, and taking careful aim, one of the Indians fell and was dragged away. Redoubling their shouts, the Indians returned with brands of fire, but another discharge, which wounded their leader, finally repelled them, leaving Sergeant Williams victor, and his aged father and mother rescued from death.

"THE LITTLE BLACK-EYED REBEL."

Mary Redmond was the daughter of a patriot of Philadelphia of some local distinction, and had many relatives who were loyalists. These were accustomed to call her "the little black-eyed rebel," so ready was she to assist the women whose husbands were fighting for freedom in procuring intelligence. The dispatches were usually sent from their friends by a boy who carried them stitched in the back of his coat. He came into the city bringing provisions to market. One morning when there was some reason to fear he was suspected, and his movements were watched by the enemy, Mary undertook to get the papers from him in safety. She went, as usual, to the market, and in a pretended game of romps, threw her shawl over the boy's head and secured the prize. She hastened with them to her anxious friends, who read them by stealth, after the windows had been carefully closed. When the Whig women in her neighborhood heard of Burgoyne's surrender, and were exulting in secret, the cunning little "rebel," prudently refraining from any open demonstration of joy, put her head up the chimney and gave a shout for Gates.

COURAGE OF A COUNTRY GIRL.

In December, 1777, while Washington was at Valley Forge and the enemy was in Philadelphia, Major Tallmadge was stationed between the two places with a detachment of cavalry, to make observations and to limit the range of British foragers. On one occasion, while performing this duty, he was informed that a country girl had gone into Philadelphia—perhaps by Washington's instigation— ostensibly to sell eggs, but really and especially to obtain information respecting the enemy; and curiosity led him to move his detachment to Germantown. There the main body halted while he advanced with a small party toward the British lines. Dismounting at a tavern in plain sight of their outposts, he soon saw a young girl coming out of the city. He watched her till she came up to the tavern; made himself known to her, and was about to receive some valuable intelligence when he was informed that the British light-horse were advancing. Stepping to the door he saw them in full pursuit of his patroles. He hastily mounted, but before he had started his chargers the girl was at his side begging for protection. Quick as thought, he ordered her to mount behind him. She obeyed, and in that way rode to Germantown, a distance of three miles. During the whole ride she remained unmoved, and never once complained of fear, although there was considerable firing of pistols, and not a little wheeling and charging.

STERLING'S BRAVERY.

While the battle of Long Island was in progress, a brave officer named Sterling, with his regiment of Maryland, and one of Delaware, were at one time left alone in the field. For nearly four hours they had stood in their ranks with colors flying; when Sterling, finding himself without hope of re-enforcement, and perceiving the main body of the British army rapidly coming behind him, gave them the word to retreat. They withdrew in perfect order; twenty marines, who mistook the Delawares, from the facing of their uniforms, for Hessians, were brought off as prisoners. The only avenue of escape was by wading through Gowamis creek; and this passage was almost cut off by troops under Cornwallis, who had advanced by the post road, and with the 2d regiment of Grenadiers and the 71st of Highlanders blocked the retreat at a house near the tide-mills, within less than half a mile of the American lines. Sterling had not a moment to deliberate; he must hold Cornwallis in check, or his whole party is lost; with the quick inspiration of disinterested valor, he ordered the Delaware regiment and one half of that of Maryland to make the best of their way across the marsh and creek; while, to secure them time for this movement, he confronted the advancing British with only five companies of Marylanders. His heroic self-sacrifice animated the young soldiers whom he retained with almost invincible resolution; they flew at the enemy with "unparalleled bravery, in view of all the American generals and troops within the lines, who alternately praised and pitied them." Washington wrung his hands as he exclaimed: "My God! what brave men must I lose this day!" They seemed likely to drive back the foremost ranks of the British; and when forced to give way, rallied and renewed the onset. In this manner ten minutes were gained, so that the Delawares, with their prisoners, and all of the Maryland regiment, but its five devoted companies, succeeded in reaching the creek. Seven were drowned in its deep waters; the rest got safely over, and were escorted to the camp by a regiment and a company, which Washington had sent out to their relief. Sterling and the few with him attempted to pass between Cornwallis and an American fort, but were beaten back by masses of troops. Pressed by the enemy in the front and the rear, attacked on the right flank and on the left, they gave up the contest. Most of them retreating to the right through the woods, were cut to pieces, or taken; nine only succeeded in crossing the creek. Sterling himself, refusing to surrender to the British general, sought Von Huister, and gave up his sword to the veteran.

A NOBLE EXPLOIT.

During the year 1780, Thomas Bennett and his son, a lad, in a field not far from their house, in Kingston, were seized and made prisoners by six Indians. Lebbeus Hammond, who had been captured a few hours before, they found tied as they entered a gorge of the mountain. Hammond had been in the battle, and was then taken prisoner. He was a prize of more than ordinary value. No doubt could exist but that he was destined a victim to the cruelist barbarity. While on their march they met two parties of Indians and Tories, descending for pillage and murder upon the settlement. A man by the name of Moses Mount, whom they knew, was particular in his inquiries into the state of the garrison and the situation of the inhabitants. To a request from Mr. Bennett, of the chief, to lend him an awl to put on a button, the savage, with a significant look, replied, "No want button for one night," and refused his request. The purpose of the Indians could not be mistaken. Whispering to Hammond, while the Indians went to a spring near by to drink, it was resolved to make an effort to escape. To stay was certain death; they could but die. Tired with their heavy march, after a supper of venison, the Indians lay around the fire, Hammond and the boy tied between them, except an old Indian who was set to keep the first watch. His spear lay by his side, while he picked the meat from the head of a deer, as half-sleeping and nodding he sat over the fire. Bennett was allowed to sit near him, and seemingly in a careless manner, took the spear, and rolled it playfully on his thigh. Watching his opportunity when least on his guard, he thrust the spear through the Indian's side, who fell with a startling groan upon the burning logs. There was not a moment to be lost. Age forgot its decrepitude. In an instant Hammond and young Bennett were cut loose, the arms seized, three of the remaining savages tomahawked, and slain as they slept, and another wounded. One only escaped unhurt. The next day the captive victors came in with five rifles, a silver mounted hanger, and several spears and blankets, as trophies of their brilliant exploit.

KADY BROWNELL.

The annals of our great war for the Union are not wanting in instances where the wife of the soldier has gone with her husband, experienced all the hardships of the camp, stood in the line with sword at her side, carried the colors into the thickest of the fight, and then when the bloody work was over, devoted herself, with the delicate tenderness of her sex, to mitigating the horrors of the battlefield. Such was the brave young wife of Robert S. Brownell; such her bearing and her services on the plains of Manassas and at the battle of Newbern, where she was the heroine.

After the colors were run down the flag mast at Fort Sumter, the First Rhode Island infantry was soon full to overflowing, having responded to the first call for troops. It had eleven full companies of one hundred each; and as ten were enough for a complete organization, a company of sharp-shooters was formed of the eleventh, and the wife of the orderly was made the color-bearer of the company. Not desiring to be a mere ornamental appendage to the company, she practiced with both rifle and sword until she became one of the best marksmen and swords-women. During one engagement word reached her that her husband had been wounded; she ran to the spot and found his injuries but slight. Going out where the dead and wounded were lying thick along the breast-works, to get blankets that would no longer do them any good, in order to make her husband and others more comfortable, here she saw several lying helpless in the mud and shallow water of the yard. These she helped up, and assisted them to get to dryer ground. From the middle of March to the last of April she remained in Newbern, nursing her husband, who for some time grew worse, and needed constant care and skillful nursing to save his life. When not over him she was doing all she could for other sufferers. Every day she contrived to save a bucket of coffee and a pail of delicate soup, and would take it over and give it out with her own hands to the wounded in the Confederate hospital. Her husband was finally removed to New York, but it was eighteen months before he touched ground; and then his surgeons pronounced him unfit for active service. As his soldier days were over, Kady had no other thought of anything more but the plain duties of the loving wife and the kind friend.

A DEVOTED LOVER.

Romantic indeed is the story of the Wisconsin girl, who, with a devotion of which only woman is capable, followed her soldier-lover through four years of active service, in the late war, and at last closed his eyes in death in a Washington hospital a few days after Lee's surrender. Her name was Ellen Goodridge, and the brave boy she loved so truly was James Hendrick. He volunteered for three months when the war broke out in 1861, and was at the first battle of Bull Run. Receiving a lieutenant's commission, he enlisted for three years, and wrote to that effect to his parents, and also to Ellen. When she told her parents that she had made up her mind to go with her lover, and share the fortunes of war by his side, they were so incensed at what they considered her folly, that they turned her from their doors, and bade her never return. Going to Washington, she found young Hendrick's regiment, and obtained permission to remain at the colonel's headquarters and look after the cooking. They were in nearly every great battle that was fought in Virginia, and in the intervals she often went with him in skirmishes and raids; on one such occasion receiving a painful wound in her arm from a minnie ball. His health remained good till after the fall of Richmond. Then he became very sick, and was taken to Washington, where she watched over his couch, bathed his hot forehead, read to him, wrote for him, and showed the most painful anxiety for his recovery; but all in vain. A day or two before he died, their marriage was solemnized by an Episcopal clergyman. The occasion was inexpressibly sad, he writhing in the grasp of a fatal disease; having survived all the great battles of the war, only to die and leave the noble girl who had been so true to him, broken-hearted, and a widow, and she almost wild with the terrible thought, that after giving up so much, and suffering so much to be near him, death would leave her only his name and a bleeding heart.

SPIRITED CONDUCT OF MRS. PHELPS.

John F. Phelps, a loyal Missourian, residing near Wilson's Creek, when the bloody engagement took place in which General Lyon met his untimely but heroic [death, was absent from home at the time of the battle, in command of a Union regiment of Missouri volunteers. After Lyon's death the Union force retreated to Springfield, leaving the body of their general in the hands of the enemy. Mrs. Phelps determined to rescue it and see that it had a Christian burial; it was reported also that some of the confederates had threatened to cut out the heart of the dead soldier and preserve it as a trophy. Arming herself, she went out on the field—appalling as it was with the dead still unburied—and stood guard over the body of the hero all night. When ordered to give it up, she fearlessly refused; and when they insisted she said they must sacrifice her before they could lay ruthless hands on the remains of that fallen hero. After daylight she made the proper arrangements, and removed the corpse to her house, where it was duly laid out. To furnish him a funeral pall, she cut into breadths and sewed together in a proper form a magnificent black velvet robe, a part of her own apparel. Though perfectly aware of her unprotected situation, the confederates surrounded the house in which the lifeless form of a gallant enemy was guarded by a solitary but heroic woman, and made the night hideous by savage screams, horrible oaths, and barbarous threats. In a short time, however, they retreated, and the body of General Lyon was taken in charge by the loyal army, removed to Connecticut, his native state, and there interred with the fullest military honors. General Price soon after returned to the vicinity of Wilson's Creek, and called on Mrs. Phelps; he was about to enter the house when she forbade his crossing her threshold. He remonstrated with her, and tried to cajole her by flattery and amusing talk; when he again spoke of coming in, she addressed him in these words: "General Price, you are a man at the head of twenty thousand troops. I am a helpless woman; you are armed; I am not; you have the physical power to take possession of my house; if you ever enter here, it will be simply by reason of my weakness, not by my consent. I ask you, as a soldier, whether you will use violence in such a case?" Thus appealed to, Price did not insist, and whenever he came there, stood in the yard and conversed with the lady of the house through the open door.

MRS. ISABELLA FOGG.

On the last day of May, 1861, came the bloody field of Fair Oaks, after which there was a broad and unbroken stream of the wounded and sick pouring steadily to the rear from the more active and warlike front; to these Mrs. Fogg administered. When asked whether she was willing to go up to the front and labor, she replied promptly, "That is just where I would like to go." A branch of the sanitary commission was accordingly established two miles from the front; and during the long, hot days of June, Mrs. Fogg was here laboring throughout the day, protecting herself from sun-stroke by a wet towel worn in her hat, distributing cooling drinks, food, and stimulants to the sick as they arrived in long trains from Fair Oaks, and as they were collected from all parts of the great army. Her labors continued until the close of war, when she was solaced and penetrated with deep gratitude to God that he so long preserved her health and strength to witness the triumph of the right, and the dawn of peace, and the day when the patriot, no longer languishing in camp nor agonizing on the field, will not suffer for what woman in her tenderness can do for him.

ANDREW JACKSON

Perhaps the greatest measure of success always follows a determination of purpose. The guiding principle of Andrew Jackson was, " Ask nothing but what is right—submit to nothing wrong." It was an abiding principle in his character from his earliest youth until the close of his life. That noble motive was the key to his great success in whatever he undertook, and is worthy of adoption by every young man when he sets out on the perilous voyage of active life. He received a fair education, for his mother designed him for the Christian ministry. But his studies were interrupted by the tumult of the on-coming Revolution, and soon after the fall of Charleston the Waxhaw settlement became a terrible scene of blood in the massacre of Buford's regiment by the fiery Tarleton. Every element of the lion in young Jackson's nature was aroused by this event, and boy as he was, not yet fourteen years of age, he joined the patriot army and went to the field. One of his brothers was killed at Stone, and himself and another brother were made captives in 1781. The widow was soon bereaved of all her family but Andrew, and after making a journey of mercy to Charleston to relieve the sick prisoners, she fell by the wayside, and the place of her sepulchre is not known unto this day. He now entered a romantic and interesting career. Finally marrying, he occupied numerous positions of public trust and affluence. His administration as president was marked by great energy, and never were the affairs of the republic, in domestic and foreign relations, more prosperous than at the close of his second term of office. The memory of this great and good man is revered by his countrymen, next to that of Washington, and to him has been awarded the first equestrian statue in bronze ever erected in this country.

DEWITT CLINTON.

From early manhood, the efforts of Mr. Clinton were directed to the elevation of his fellow-men. Throughout his long political career he was the earnest and steadfast friend of education and the rights of men. His powerful mind was brought to bear with great vigor upon the subject of legislative aid in furtherance of popular education, and also the abolition of human slavery in New York. Some of the noblest institutions for the promotion of art, literature, science and benevolence in that city were founded under his auspices. The two objects of his life were the advancement of his fellow-men and the establishment of a canal between Lake Erie and the Hudson River. This was finally established, and his most enduring monument is the Erie canal, whose bosom has borne sufficient food to appease the hunger of the whole earth, and poured millions of treasure into the coffers of the State.

JOSEPH WARREN.

Prominent among the Revolutionary patriots was the subject of the present sketch. When he died the patriot cause sustained a severe blow. Patriotism was a ruling emotion of his heart, and he never lacked boldness to express his opinions freely. He was extremely efficient in fostering a spirit of national liberty and independence among the people. His suggestive mind planned many daring schemes in secret caucus, and he was ever ready to lead in the execution of any measures for resisting the encroachments of imperial power. He delivered the first annual oration on the subject of the "Boston Massacre," in 1771, and in 1775 he solicited the honor of performing the perilous service again, because some British officers had menaced the life of any one who should attempt it. The "Old South" was crowded, and the aisles, stairs, and pulpit were filled with British soldiers full armed. The intrepid young orator entered by a window, spoke fearlessly in the presence of those bayonets which seemed alive with threats, of the early struggle of the colonies of New England, and then, in sorrowful tones and deep pathos of expression, told of the wrongs and oppressions under which they were then suffering. Even the soldiers wept; and thus the young hero, firm in the faith that "resistance to tyrants is obedience to God," triumphed, and fearlessly bearded the lion in his den. He was killed while urging the American forces forward at Bunker Hill. Where his body fell the great Bunker Hill monument now stands. Congress expressed its sorrow by resolutions, and its gratitude by ordering that "his eldest son should be educated at the expense of the United States." Congress also ordered a monument to be erected.

MRS. THOMAS HEYWARD.

The firmness of this lady is well worthy of admiration. An order having been issued for a general illumination, to celebrate the supposed victory at Guilford, the front of the house occupied by Mrs. Heyward and her sister, Mrs. George Abbot Hall, remained in darkness. Indignant at so decided a mark of disrespect, an officer forced his way into her presence, and sternly demanded of Mrs. Heyward, "how dare you disobey the order which has been issued; why, madam, is not your house illuminated?" "Is it possible for me, sir," replied the lady with perfect calmness, "to feel a spark of joy? Can I celebrate the victory of your army, while my husband remains a prisoner at St. Augustine?" "That," replied the officer, "is a matter of little consequence; the last hopes of rebellion are crushed by the defeat of Greene; you *shall* illuminate." "Not a single light," replied the lady, "shall be placed by my consent, on such an occasion, in any window of the house." "Then, madam, I will return with a party, and before midnight level it to the ground." "You have power to destroy, sir, and seem well disposed to use it, but over my opinions you possess no control. I disregard your menaces, and resolutely declare, *I will not illuminate.*"

MRS. HETTY M. McEWEN.

Nashville, Tennessee, was the only city in the seceding states that contained a large number of genuine Unionists, who had the courage to assert their sentiments openly and in defiance of southern sympathizers. This fearlessness was as often manifested by women as by men. The southern character, frank, ardent and uncalculating, was never more aptly illustrated than by the high-spirited defiance with which they dared all danger and all criticism in manifesting fidelity to the Union. During the spring and summer of 1861, while Isham G. Harris and his co-traitors were plotting dishonor and disaster for Tennessee, and a majority in the middle and western districts sympathized with him, there were a few in Nashville who frankly characterized his conduct in no measured terms, and advertised their sentiments by keeping the national colors always flying from their house-tops. Of these few, Mrs. Hetty M. McEwen was perhaps the most conspicuous, and her conduct in defense of the flag upon her house is truly memorable. She was born during the presidency of George Washington, and had six uncles at the battle of King's Mountain, four of whom wet that hard fought field with their life-blood. Her husband, Colonel Robert H. McEwen, fought under Jackson at Horseshoe, and his father was a surgeon in the Revolutionary army. She could remember the time when there was no Tennesseean that did not live in a log cabin, no preacher that did not take his rifle into the pulpit with him as regularly as his Bible, and was as familiar with one as with the other. When secession was talked of, with her own fingers she stitched together the folds of bunting, and reared the red, white and blue on a flag-staff in the yard of the residence that had been known as theirs almost from the time when Nashville was an Indian fort. As treason grew less and less odious, the flag was subjected to various insults. Boys threw stones at it. The papers noticed it, and advised its removal. Colonel McEwen received an anonymous letter full of plantation venom, and threatening assassination unless the odious colors were removed. When at length the machinations of Governor Harris culminated, and Tennessee was made to appear of secession preferences by forty thousand majority, Colonel McEwen fastened a pole into one of his chimneys, and nailed the national colors where they could float solitary, yet dauntless and defiant, over the rebellion-cursed city. The hostility now became fiercer than ever. He was told that the flag must come down from the roof if they had to fire the house to bring it down. He asked his wife what they had better do about the flag, adding that he would sustain her in any course she thought best to adopt. "Load me the shot gun, Colonel McEwen," said the heroic old lady. And he loaded it for her with sixteen buckshots in each barrel. "Now," added she, "I will take the responsibility of guarding that flag. Whoever attempts to pass my door on their way to the roof for that star-spangled banner, under which my four uncles fell at King's Mountain, must go over my dead body." Not long after, Governor Harris issued an order for all fire-arms to be brought to him at the state house, and enforced it by sending a squad of soldiers to Colonel McEwen's house. In reply to their demands, she said, "Go tell your master, the governor, that I will not surrender my gun to any one but himself, and if he wants it, to come in person and risk the circumstances."

AN INSTANCE OF SELF-SACRIFICE.

When the lines of field works were being established around the national capital, the military engineers in charge of their location came upon a lovely spot near Bladensburg, Maryland. A tasteful cottage home, standing on the verge of a gentle slope, was surrounded by orchard shade trees, grape-vines, a charming flower garden, a lawn of exquisite smoothness, and "shrubberies that a Shenstone might have envied." This little paradise was the residence of a lady and her daughters, whose husband and father was away fighting under the Union flag. The formation of the country was such as to require the line of earthworks to pass directly through these beautiful grounds and gardens. The position commands the country around for miles, and was the proper place for a battery. Yet the officers saw at a glance that the planting of guns on the hill would make terrible havoc of that charming rural home. Every tree in the orchard must come down, the shrubbery be torn away, a wide ditch cut through the flower garden, and the whole place, in fact, desolated and ruined. Other lines were run in the hope of avoiding this hill entirely, but in vain. No other eminence afforded such a tactical position, and to neglect it might be to throw the advantage thus afforded into the hands of the enemy. It became the unpleasant duty of the officers in charge of the survey to call on the lady and inform her of the military necessity that demanded the mutilation of her grounds, and the destruction of all that was loveliest on the premises. They stated their conclusion in as delicate a manner as possible, and told her how they had hoped to avoid an occupation of her land. She heard their statements in silence, arose, walked to the window, and gazed for a few moments on the tender lawn and the blooming garden. Then, with tearful eyes, she turned to the engineer and said, "If it must be so, take it freely. I had hoped to live here in peace and quiet, and never to leave this sweet spot, which my husband has taken so much delight in making beautiful. But if my country demands it, take it freely. You have my consent." When the women of Tyre cut their long hair and braided it into bow-strings for the archers on the walls of the besieged city, their devotion was no greater than was here shown by the patriotic lady of Bladensburg.

BENJAMIN PIERCE.

The career of Benjamin Pierce, the father of the fourteenth President of the United States, affords a noble example of true manhood in private and public life, which the young men of our republic ought to study and imitate. It is an example of perseverance in well-doing for self, friends, and country, being rewarded by a conscience void of offense, a long life, and the love and honor of fellow-men. In these lies hidden the priceless pearl of earthly happiness.

He was left fatherless at the age of six years, and was placed under the guardianship of a paternal uncle. His opportunities for education were small, but the lad, possessing a naturally vigorous intellect, improved those opportunities with parsimonious assiduity. His body was invigorated by farm labor; and when, at the age of seventeen years, the first gun of the Revolution at Lexington echoed among the New England hills, and he armed for the battle-fields of freedom, young Pierce was fitted, morally and physically, for a soldier of the truest stamp. He hastened to Lexington, pushed on to Cambridge, and six days after the retreat of the British troops from Concord he was enrolled in Captain Ford's company as a regular soldier. He fought bravely on Breed's Hill seven weeks afterward; was faithful in camp and on guard until the British were driven from Boston in the spring of 1776; followed the fortunes of Washington during the ensuing campaigns of that year, and was orderly sergeant of his company before he was twenty years of age, in the glorious conflict which resulted in the capture of Burgoyne at Saratoga, in the autumn of 1777. His valor there won for him the commission of ensign. The young man who bore that commission and the American flag, in the hottest of the fight, was killed. Young Pierce rushed forward, seized the banner, and bore it triumphantly to the American lines, amid the shouts of his companions. The war left young Pierce as it found him, a true patriot, but penniless, for the Continental paper-money in which he had been paid had become worthless. Yet he was rich in the glorious experience of endurance under hardships; and entering the service of a large landholder, it was not long before he owned a small tract of land in the southern part of Hillsborough, New Hampshire, whereon he built a log hut, and commenced a clearing, in the spring of 1786. He was unmarried, and lived alone. Labor sweetened his coarse food and deepened his slumbers. He cultivated social relations with the scattered population around him; and in the autumn of 1786 the governor of New Hampshire appointed him brigade-major of his district. His public services were of the highest order. We cannot too reverently cherish the remembrance of such a man.

BRAVE MRS. HURD.

When the call "to arms" was heard throughout this vast land in 1861, the troops of regulars then stationed along the western frontier, forming a line of steel between the treacherous Indians and the inhabitants of the plains and valleys, who came bringing with them the arts of civilization, were called to the East for active service. This gave rise to a series of atrocities and murders which recall the old story of Wyoming.

About the 17th of August, a party of two hundred and fifty or more Indians proceeded to the agency at Yellow Medicine, and commenced an indiscriminate slaughter of all the whites. The marauders, flushed with success, pressed on with their work of death, murdering with the most atrocious brutalities the settlers in their isolated farm-houses. The story told by Mrs. Hurd is as pitiable as it is harrowing. Her husband had left her and her two children to go to Dakota; they were then living about one hundred miles west of Mankota, on the Missouri river; the Indians were plenty, but friendly. After Mr. Hurd had been away about two months the wife became very anxious. One morning about twenty Indians rode up to the house, and Mrs. Hurd recognized one of the horses as belonging to her husband when he started on his trip. The Indians went in and commenced to light their pipes and smoke; Mr. Voight, a hired man, carried the baby, who became frightened, into the yard, when one of the Indians shot him through the back. At this signal, ten or fifteen more Indians and squaws rushed into the house and began to destroy everything they could lay their hands on. The Indians told her to leave with her children, and they would not kill her; they accompanied her about three miles of the distance and then left her. For several days she wandered hopelessly about, not knowing the road, and having nothing with which to feed her starving and crying children. The cries of her offspring nerved her, and she went on. Coming upon a house, she promised them food, but it was tenantless and nothing could be found to stimulate their tired bodies. She says: To my great delight, however, I found the remains of a spoiled ham; here, I may say my good fortune began. There was no more of it than a pound—and that much decayed—and I saved this for my boy, feeding it to him in very small quantities; he ceased vomiting and revived rapidly. About eight o'clock on the morning of the third day, I again set forth on my weary road for the residence of Mr. Brown, twenty-five miles distant, and reached it in two days. When almost there, two of our old neighbors overtook us, under the escort of the mail carrier; both of them had been wounded by the Indians, and left for dead. Arriving at Mr. Brown's house, we remained there ten days, living on potatoes and green corn. A party of twelve men with a wagon were sent to our relief, and we were made comfortable; but the sad and sickening thought was now fully confirmed in my mind, that my husband had been killed in the general massacre of all the remote settlements, and my fatherless children and myself left beggars. Our heroine bore her two children during a part of her fearful flight, but having been without food for nearly sixty hours, and all the time sustaining the little one on her arm by food from her own bosom was compelled to deposit half her precious cargo in the grass, and return for the other; thus, on the two days when she traveled, advancing twelve miles each day, herself walking thirty-six. Could the force of nature go farther? Do our annals anywhere contain a more remarkable instance of the wonderful sustaining power which maternal love can inspire in the delicate frame of woman?

JOSEPH REED.

In these days of bribe taking and giving, when political influence and power are so often purchased, the sterling words of Joseph Reed come to us: "I am not worth purchasing, but such as I am, the King of Great Britain is not rich enough to do it." These were the noble words which tradition attributes to him, when a bribe was offered for his influence in favor of Great Britain, in 1778. He was a member of congress when commissions came from England in 1778, to negotiate a peace on the basis of submission of the colonists to the crown. It was to the agent of one of these commissioners that he is said to have addressed the words above quoted. The fact became known, and congress refused further intercourse with the commissioners. In 1778 General Reed was chosen president of the newly-organized commonwealth of Pennsylvania, and filled that station with great ability. Like all dutiful men, he was the target for unmeasured abuse from his political oponents; but when time dissipated the clouds of party rancor, all men beheld in Joseph Reed a patriot and an honest man.

MARGARET E. BRECKENRIDGE.

Self-sacrificing devotion to duty, and disinterested heroism, are always to be admired in either men or women. During the disheartening siege of Vicksburg, two ladies were standing on the deck of a steamer, in the rear of the beleaguered city. One present chided the unusually slender figure who was foremost in her heroic self forgetfulness, by saying, "You must hold back, you are going beyond your strength; you will die if you are not more prudent." Instantly the dark eyes of our present subject glittered with the intense enthusiasm of her soul, as, with a voice of impressive earnestness, she exclaimed, "Well, what if I do! Shall men come here by tens of thousands, and fight, and suffer, and die, and shall not some women be willing to die to sustain and succor them?"

In April, 1862, Miss Breckenridge left her home in Princeton for the West, and with the full intention of devoting herself to the soldiers for the war. She labored in Baltimore, Lexington, Ky., and St. Louis, visiting the hospitals and performing like missions of mercy.

"Ma'am," said a fair boy of seventeen summers, as she smoothed his hair and told him, with glistening eyes, he would soon see his mother and the old homestead, and be won back to life and health, "where do you come from? How could you come way down here to take care of us poor, sick, dirty boys?"

She said, "I consider it an honor to wait on you and wash off the mud you have waded through for me."

Her attention in the wards was constant, even when death was lurking in her enfeebled system. With her little Testament in her hand, she went from one bedside to another, an administering angel to all there, cheering the desponding, encouraging the timid and doubtful. At twilight it was her custom to sing hymns in the wards, and long after she had died her sweet voice was spoken of as a blessing lost by the sick and suffering. When the frail tenement of her soaring spirit was tottering, the greatest desire that she expressed was to recover, that she might labor till the war was over. Her memory is still fragrant among the soldiers and loyal people in the border states; she stirred them up to increased labor, and the mention of her name and allusion to her death bring forth tears from those who only saw and heard her once, for they loved her.

BRAVE BOY SOLDIERS.

Soon after the capture of one of the Confederate forts in the West, a lady went into the hospital where the wounded had been taken. She was much attracted by two young men, lying side by side, all splintered and bandaged so that they could not move hand or foot, but so cheerful and happy looking that she said, "Why, boys, you look very bright, to-day." "Oh, yes," they said, "we're all right now. We've been turned this morning." And she found that for six long weeks they had lain in one position, and for the first time that morning had been moved to the other side of their cot. "And were you," she asked, "among those poor boys who were left lying where you fell that bitter morning till you froze fast to the ground?" "Yes, ma'am," they said, "We were lying there two days. You know they had no time to attend to us; they had to go and take the fort." "And didn't you think it was cruel in them to leave you to suffer so long?" "Why, no, ma'am, we wanted them to go and take the fort." "But when they took it, you were in too much agony to know or care for it?" "Oh, no, ma'am!" they answered, with flashing eyes and faces glowing with the recollections of that day, "there were a whole lot of us wounded fellows on the hillside, watching to see if they would get the fort. When we saw they had it, every one of us that had a whole arm waved it in the air, and we hurrahed till the air rang again."

MRS. ELIDA RUMSEY FOWLE.

Just liberated from the famous tobacco house in Richmond, now known as Libby prison, and standing within shelter of the national capital, for the preservation of which they had fought and suffered long, a band of dirty, haggard soldiers once stood, indifferent almost to their present surroundings. Presently a clerk from the navy department found his way among them, and inquired whether they would like to hear a song. "Oh, very well, I guess," was the somewhat languid reply. He soon returned with a young lady, who sang the first stanza of "Star Spangled Banner." Charmed by her powers, they formed a circle around her, and when those on the outside complained that they could not see, some one said, "Make a stand for her." Fifty knapsacks at once were placed in position, and she ascended, completing the national hymn. She saw a mission before her. While she could not take the sword or bayonet, there was good for her to do in soothing, cheering and sustaining the soldiers. From that time on, till after the battle of Gettysburg, and near the close of the war, Miss Rumsey devoted herself to labors for the good, the comfort, the social, moral and mental well-being of the soldier. Near her father's house were located several hospitals. Upon these she was a constant visitor. On Sabbath afternoons, and often during the week, she, in company with Mr. Fowle and other Christian gentlemen, visited various hospitals and held soldiers' prayer meetings in different wards, singing the most familiar and widely-known songs of religious love and worship. The soldiers free library on Judiciary Square, in Washington, was established mainly through the efforts of Mr. Fowle and Miss Rumsey. At times Washington City contained as many as twenty thousand sick, wounded, or convalescent soldiers. For these, papers, magazines, and all sorts of valuable and entertaining, yet moral books, were secured. In a little more than a year they distributed two thousand three hundred and seventy-one Bibles and Testaments, almost two thousand books and magazines, forty thousand tracts, thirty-five thousand papers, twenty-five reams of writing paper, nine thousand envelopes, and of "creature comforts," over three thousand shirts and drawers, great quantities of towels, sheets, gowns, slippers, wines and jellies. They also gave numerous concerts to raise money to erect the library building. Two concerts realized them about three hundred dollars. Both Houses granted ground for the erection of the proposed building. Other concerts were now given, and soon a building sixty-five feet long, and twenty-four wide, was erected and dedicated to the free use of soldiers. Before the close of the war there were six thousand volumes of good reading matter on the shelves of the institution. Just after the second battle of Bull Run, Mr. Fowle obtained an ambulance, and Miss Rumsey loaded it with some four hundred and fifty loaves of bread, together with a large supply of other necessaries. They left Washington and drove to Centreville, halting at a little building near the road, which was already almost full of wounded. The stacks of wounded were laid upon all sides of the room, and the blood which flowed from so many open veins ran down and stood in a crimson pool all over the middle of the room. Most of them had eaten nothing for twenty-four hours. Having fed them she went inside to do whatever she might to relieve their sufferings. She was soon overcome with the ghastly sight, smell of blood and moanings of the wounded. Becoming unconscious, she fell over as helpless as those she was relieving. When she regained self-possession she chided herself—"To think that I have come all the way from Washington to bind up the wounds of these soldiers, and here the first case of running blood I see I have to become faint and helpless; I will go back and work, for I'm determined to accomplish something." A dying soldier, by whose side Miss Rumsey sat, said to her, " Will you, kind lady, write to Miss ———, to whom I have been engaged for the past two years, and break to her the sad news?" A few moments afterward he added, in a clear but faint voice, "Tell Denning," a wounded comrade from the same town, "if he gets well, to tell my friends that I was wounded bravely fighting for my country, and die happy." A lasting benediction rests upon her work and labors. In the spring of 1863, after the completion of the sailors' free library, and as there was much less demand for constant hospital labor, Miss Rumsey was united for life with Mr. Fowle, who labored constantly and most effectively with Miss Rumsey for the physical and moral well-being of the soldier. They had acquired a national reputation by their humane work, and their marriage was celebrated in the House of Representatives. The blessings this brave couple have done can never be estimated, but the lesson to us is "Go ye, and do likewise."

BRAVERY OF MISS SCHWARTZ.

In the summer of 1863 a party of guerillas went in the night to the house of Mr. Schwartz, twelve miles from Jefferson City, Missouri, and on demanding admittance, were refused by Miss Schwartz, a girl of fifteen years. They answered that they would come in, and commenced breaking down the door. Five or six men, who were in the house, now ran out the back-door, taking with them, as they supposed, all the fire-arms. In their haste a revolver was left, which the heroic girl seized, and pointing it at the head of the leader of the gang, said, "Come on if you want to; some of you shall fall, or I will!" They then said they would kill her if she did not leave the door. She answered, "The first man of you that takes a step toward this door dies. This is the home of my parents, my brothers and sisters, and I am able to and shall defend it." After a brief consultation the ruffians left.

THADDEUS KOSCIUSCZKO.

Although a foreigner, the deeds of this great man in America have been such as to naturalize him. In early manhood he eloped with a young lady of rank and fortune, was pursued and overtaken by her proud father, and was driven to the alternative of killing the parent or abandoning the maid. He chose the latter and went to Paris. He came, in the summer of 1776, to America, and presented himself to Washington. "What can you do?" asked the commander-in-chief. "Try me," was the laconic reply. Washington was pleased with the young man, made him his aid, and in October of that year, the Continental Congress gave him the appointment of engineer in the army. In the Polish campaign against Russia, in 1792, Kosciusczko greatly distinguished himself; and in the noble attempt of his countrymen, in 1794, to regain their lost liberty, he was chosen general-in-chief. Soon afterward, at the head of four thousand men, he defeated twelve thousand Russians. Invested with the powers of a military dictator, he boldly defied the combined armies of Russia and Prussia, amounting to more than one hundred and fifty thousand men. At length success deserted him; and in October, 1794, his troops were overpowered in a battle about fifty miles from Warsaw. He was wounded, fell from his horse, and was made prisoner, exclaiming, "The end of Poland!"

In the summer of 1797 Kosciusczko visited America, and was received with distinguished honors. Congress awarded him a life pension, and gave him a tract of land for his revolutionary services. On the 16th of October, 1817, that noble patriot died, at the age of sixty-one years. His body was buried in the tomb of the ancient kings of Poland, at Cracow, with great pomp; and at Warsaw there was a public funeral in his honor. The Senate of Cracow decreed that a lofty mound should be erected to his memory on the heights of Bronislawad; and for three years men of every class and age toiled in the erection of that magnificent cairn, three hundred feet in height. The cadets of the military academy at West Point, on the Hudson, erected an imposing monument there to the memory of Kosciusczko, in 1829, at a cost of five thousand dollars. His most enduring monument is the record of his deeds on the pages of history.

MRS. MARY W. LEE.

This name will recall to the minds of thousands of our brave soldiers who fought in the Army of the Potomac, the face and figure of a cheerful, tender-hearted woman, herself the mother of a soldier boy, who for month after month moved about the hospitals of the army, a blessing and comfort to thousands of weary sufferers. When at one time the wounded were famishing from hunger and thirst, she found a sutler, who, with enterprise that would have been becoming in anything less purely selfish, had urged his wagon well to the front, and was selling at exorbitant rates to the exhausted men. She took money from her private purse and again and again bought his bread and soft crackers at his army rates. At last such repeated proofs of generosity touched the heart of the army shylock, and he was determined not to be outdone so entirely by a woman. About the third or fourth time she pulled out her purse he exclaimed, "Great God, I can't stand this any longer. Give that woman the bread!" The ice was now broken, and from giving to her, he began to give away, himself, till his last cracker had gone down the throat of a half-famished hero, and he drove away with his wagon lighter and his heart softer for having met a noble-hearted woman. Among the fatally wounded was one named Adams, from the Nineteenth Massachusetts, whose brother brought him to Mrs. Lee, and said: "My good lady, my brother here will die, I think ; the regiment is ordered to Harper's Ferry; will you promise to look after him, and when he dies to see that he is decently buried, and mark the spot so that I can find his body and take it on to our home in Massachusetts?" Mrs. Lee promised the heavy-hearted soldier that all his wishes should be respected, and he buckled on his sword and marched on to the front. A few days after he sought out Mrs. Lee, and she gave him a full account of the last hours of his brother and his dying words, and then taking him out among the thick and fresh heaped mounds, pointed out a grave better rounded than the rest, and distinctly marked, and told him his brother was buried there, and so he found it. Such was the fidelity and perfect reliability at all times and in all trusts committed to her. Sometimes, just as the hospital had become composed for the night, and the old campaign stove had grown cold for the first time in eighteen hours, an immense train of ambulance would come rolling in from the front, all loaded down with men, sick, wounded, dusty and famishing. There was no other way but to rise, and work, perhaps, till long past midnight. It was fortunate that with such willingness of heart, and such skill, nay, such genius, as she displayed for cooking under all the disadvantages of camp life, Mrs. Lee had also a robust constitution and excellent health, otherwise she must have broken down under the long-continued labors and sleeplessness of that last grand campaign against Richmond. Into such womanly duties she carried the rich consciousness of having given herself up entirely, for three laborious but happy years, to the exercise of heavenly charities, and to the practice of that mercy that is twice blessed.

THOMAS MACDONOUGH.

The bravery of the man whose name heads this sketch, was born of true courage, not of mere intrepidity, and he never quailed in the face of most imminent danger. He was one of the daring men selected by Decatur to assist him in burning the Philadelphia frigate, and he partook of the honors of that brilliant exploit. At the battle of Lake Champlain, on the 11th of September, 1814, Macdonough played a very important part with his little squadron of four ships and ten galleys. Macdonough, by superior nautical skill and dexterity in the management of guns, soon caused the British flag to fall, when Provost, in dismay, hastily retreated, leaving victory with the Americans on both land and water. When the British squadron appeared off Cumberland-head, Macdonough knelt on the deck of the Saratoga (his flag-ship), in the midst of his men, and prayed to the God of Battles for aid. A curious incident occurred during the engagement that soon followed. A British ball demolished a hen-coop on board the Saratoga. A cock, released from his prison, flew into the rigging and crowed lustily, at the same time flapping his wings with triumphant vehemence. The seamen regarded the event as a good omen, and they fought like tigers, while the cock cheered them on with his crowings, until the Brisish flag was struck and the firing ceased. His brilliant services and deeds were awarded by congress, and by the legislatures of several states. His fame was heralded far and wide. At about the close of the war, Commodore Macdonough's health gave way, yet he lived for more than ten years with the tooth of consumption undermining his citadel of life. He was exemplary in every relation of life, and had but few of the common faults of humanity.

NOBILITY OF CHARACTER.

Perhaps no event in the history of our nation ever called forth such unexampled bravery and nobility of character as the late Rebellion. It is said of one, Frederick Allen, from Kendall's Mills, who was very sick with typhoid pneumonia, and the doctor having administered stimulants, he refused to take anything containing alcohol, saying he had given his mother a solemn promise that he would not take any while in the army. No inducement could prevail until his father came down, and told him his mother released him from his promise, as she knew it was to save his life. He recovered health, and was in all the battles with his regiment. At Bristol Station he was ordered color guard, and the regiment captured several guns. In the battle of the Wilderness he was wounded slightly in the arm and went to the rear, but returned very soon and received a severe wound in the head, being disabled for several weeks. Returning to his regiment, he fought around Petersburg, till again attacked by typhoid pneumonia, of which he died only a few days before Lee's surrender—as brave and noble a youth as ever shouldered arms; a soldier of the cross no less than of the starry flag.

PATRIOTIC DEVOTION.

Among the many noble-minded and heroic men who fought in the late war, Major William F. Smith, of the First Delaware, was prominent. Wounded severely in the leg, he suffered amputation, and death followed. He had been severely wounded at Fredericksburg, and again at Gettysburg. When urged by his friends to expose his life less freely, "No," he would reply, "I am no better than any other soldier." They urged him to remember how much it would grieve his mother. "I know it," said he, "but I am no better than any other mother's son." When informed that he could not live, he thanked the doctors for the pains they had taken with his case: "You have done all that you could for me, but Providence has some wise end in view in overruling your efforts." His last words to his young brother were, "Kiss mother for me, Lee."

Another who sealed his devotion with his blood, was Lieutenant-Colonel John

A. Crosby, of the Sixty-first Pennsylvania volunteers. He had entered the service as orderly sergeant, was badly wounded in both hips at Fredericksburg, and afterward lost an arm fighting before Washington, in Early's last invasion. When his friends remonstrated with him for keeping the field thus mutilated, he said, " My country has had my arm. She is welcome to my life." Before leaving home for the last time, he bade his wife and family good-by, telling them he should never see them again on earth. Those who knew him best, say that no better man or braver soldier ever died for his country. He fell in the last great battle of the war, before Petersburg, in April, 1865.

JOHN JACOB ASTOR.

Boldly emblazoned upon his escutcheon, as a youth and as a man, the guiding principle of Astor's life was, "Be honest, industrious, and avoid gambling." Upon this solid moral basis he built the superstructure of his fame, and secured his great wealth. Likewise can every young man who has a high, noble, guiding purpose and aim in life. In all his mammoth business operations he was ever honest and honorable. His fur trade accumulated him mints of money, which at his death was magnanimously bestowed. The great bulk of his immense property, amounting to several millions of dollars, was left to his family. Before his death he provided ample funds for the establishment and support of a splendid public library in the city of New York; and he also gave a large sum of money to his native town, for the purpose of founding an institution for the education of the young, and as a retreat for indigent and aged persons. The Astor Library in New York, and the Astor House in Walldorf, were both opened in 1854. They are noble monuments to the memory of the "merchant prince."

MRS. JOHN HARRIS.

At the very outset of the war, before the blood had commenced to flow in the long fratricidal strife, a group of ladies in Philadelphia met and organized a system of relief for the sufferings and privations which they knew must follow in the train of the war. If there were any such vain decorations of human approbation as a crown, or a wreath, or a star for her who in that war did the most, and labored the longest, who visited the greatest number of hospitals, prayed with the greatest number of suffering and dying soldiers, penetrated nearest to the front, and underwent the greatest amount of fatigue and exposure for the soldier—that crown or that star would be rightfully given to Mrs. John Harris, of Philadelphia. Mrs. Harris was at Savage's Station and Seven Pines while the fight was raging. Here in the primary hospitals and under the trees in the rear of the carnage, she took part in scenes and assumed duties which not often fall to her sex. Now she was soothing patients under the hands of the operator; now preparing the minds " of great noble-looking men, officers and privates," to submit to the amputation of an arm or leg. Her woman's heart was much moved for a captain from Massachusetts, who pleaded very hard for his leg. "Oh, my wife and children," he would say, "it will kill them to see me so mutilated." But it was of no avail. The ball had shattered his knee-joint, and amputation was unavoidable. So the chloroform was pressed to his mouth, and he was taken insensible to the operating table. We find her at one time in Nashville, laboring with the same earnest zeal. Her system was taxed to the utmost, and finally gave way, and she was prostrated in sickness. Almost her last act of kindness to soldiers was bestowed upon the wretched victims of malignity that had staggered alive out of the infamous prison pens at Andersonville and Salisbury. When peace at last came, she went back again to her household, suffering constantly from a sun stroke received while laboring on the field at Savage's Station. But if the affectionate admiration of the thousands who saw her labors and were benefited by them, is precious—this admiration, this blessing, this reward she had to alleviate the weariness of her sick chamber.

OLIVER HAZZARD PERRY.

Always thoughtful, studious, and inquisitive on ship-board, our present hero soon became a skillful seaman and navigator. Early in 1812 he was placed in command of a flotilla of gun-boats in New York harbor. He soon became disgusted with that service, and solicited and obtained for himself and men permission to reinforce Commodore Chauncey on Lake Ontario. That officer immediately dispatched Perry to Lake Erie, to superintend the building of a small squadron there to oppose a British naval force on those western waters. When ready, Perry cruised about the west end of the lake, and on the 10th of September, 1813, he had a severe engagement with the enemy. In the Lawrence—which displayed at its mast-head the words of the hero after whom she was named, "Don't give up the ship"—Perry led the squadron, and after many acts of great skill and courage he achieved a complete victory. He was then only twenty-seven years of age. It was one of the most important events of the war. The victor was promoted to captain, received the thanks of congress and state legislatures, and was honored by his government with a gold commemorative medal. When, after cruising in the the Mediterranean sea, he returned to America and performed a deed of heroism equal to any achieved in the public service. His vessel was lying in Newport harbor, in mid-winter. During a fearful storm, intelligence reached him that a merchant vessel was wrecked upon a reef, six miles distant. He immediately manned his barge, and said to his crew, "Come, my boys, we are going to the relief of shipwrecked seamen; pull away!" and soon afterward he had rescued eleven half-exhausted men, who were clinging to the floating quarter-deck of their broken vessel. To Perry it was an act of simple duty in the cause of humanity; to his countrymen it appeared as holiest heroism, deserving of a civic crown. He lives in the hearts of his countrymen. Numerous monuments have been erected to his memory, one of which stands in the public park in Cleveland.

ISRAEL PUTNAM.

Heralds on swift relays of horses transmitted the famous war messages of April, 1775, from hand to hand, till village repeated it to village; the sea to the backwoods; the plain to the highlands; and it was never suffered to droop till it had borne north and south, east and west, throughout the land. Its loud reveille broke the rest of the trappers of New Hampshire, and ringing like bugle notes from peak to peak, overleaped the Green Mountains, swept onward to Montreal, and descended the ocean river, till the responses were echoed from the cliffs of Quebec. With one impulse the colonies sprung to arms; with one spirit they pledged themselves to each other, "to be ready for the extreme event." With one heart, the continent cried, "Liberty or death!" In Connecticut, Trumbull, the governor, sent out word to convene the legislature of the colony

at Hartford on the Wednesday following the celebrated battle of Lexington. Meantime the people could not be restrained. On the morning of the 20th, just succeeding the battle, Israel Putnam, of Pomfret, in a leather frock and apron, was assisting hired men to build a stone wall on his farm when he received the news. Leaving them to continue their task, he set off instantly to arouse the militia officers of the nearest towns. On his return, he found hundreds who had mustered and chosen him their leader. Issuing orders for them to follow, he himself pushed forward without changing his check shirt he had worn in the field, and reached Cambridge at sunrise the next morning, having ridden the same horse a hundred miles within eighteen hours. He brought to the service of his country courage which during the war was never questioned, and a heart than which none throbbed more honestly or warmly for American freedom.

MOTHER BYCKERDYKE.

Perhaps the best idea of the nature and value of the labors of Mrs. Bycker-dyke, of Illinois, during the civil war, can be given from an extract of a letter written from Chattanooga, by Mrs. Porter—another noble laborer for the soldiers —soon after the battle there. She says: " I reached this place New Year's Eve. The next morning was very cold. The wind came sweeping around Lookout Mountain, and uniting with currents from the valleys of Missionary Ridge, pressed in upon the hospital tents, overturning some, and making the inmates of all tremble with cold and anxious fear. The cold had been preceded by a great rain, which added to the general discomfort. Mrs. Byckerdyke went from tent to tent in the gale, carrying hot bricks and hot drink, to warm and to cheer the poor fellows. 'She is a power of good,' said one soldier. 'We fared mighty poor till she came here,' said another. 'God bless the sanitary commission,' said a third, 'for sending women among us.'," The soldiers fully appreciated "Mother Byckerdyke," as they called her, and her work.

MRS. MAY MORRIS HUSBAND.

One of the many hundreds whom the subject of the present sketch nursed and blessed during her long career as a hospital matron and nurse, in speaking of the thorough and unostentatious heartiness of her work, said the soldiers could account for such unselfishness only from the fact that she is the grand-daughter of Robert Morris, of revolutionary fame. Hundreds of men, scattered all over the states, will always remember and revere her. In her labors she al-ways sought such places as were farthest from ready help, and where they would be of the most use. She never seemed to care for her own comfort, disregarding the requirements of her health, never leaving her self-imposed duties till sick-ness and exhaustion drove her home for rest and quiet, and while so resting, preparing supplies to be taken to the army as soon as she was again able to re-sume her duties. A New York soldier—a mere boy—sick with fever, was discov-ered also to have diptheria in its most malignant form. He was at once removed to a tent put up for the purpose, in a distant part of the grove, away from all others, and a soldier detailed as nurse, who, however, fearing the disease, neg-lected him. Knowing this, Mrs. Husband took charge of the patient, staying every moment that could be spared from the rest of the sick, for several days and nights, tenderly caring for him like a saint; reading to him from the Testa-ment, and taking his dying message for his mother, " that she must not mourn for him, for he was willing and ready to die." She seemed to consider the soldiers as her children, and watched over them with as much tender solicitude as though they were her sons. She never appeared to think of herself; her thoughts all centered on the sick or wounded soldiers. She was only too happy to be of serv-ice to anyone in trouble. At one time she found a soldier sentenced to be shot; satisfied from what she could learn concerning his case that he was innocent of the charges brought against him, she set herself to work to save his life. Failing to make any impression at brigade, division, and corps headquarters, she, noth-

ing daunted, carried her case to army headquarters, where she met only with a re-
pulse, even from the kind-hearted Meade. Not yet discouraged, she resolved to
make one more attempt, determined to save that young man's life. She went to
Washington and finally carried her point. This is but one instance of many
similar acts. She undoubtedly saved the lives of many by her skill in dressing
wounds, and her unceasing attention. Her popularity was not the reflection of
another's fame. It was an outburst of unfeigned gratitude and real admiration
which so many had long felt for a noble and accomplished woman, whose patriotism and humanity alone had impelled her, for year after year, to follow up
the marches of our armies, on her ministry of love; to devote herself to the
welfare of suffering patriots; to know nothing of home and its sacred comforts
as long as one lonely or desponding soldier was languishing in a hospital ward.

MAJOR SAMUEL McCULLOCH.

Among the earliest settlers on Short Creek, not far from Wheeling, Virginia,
was the McCulloch family, composed of three brothers, Abraham, Samuel, and
John, and two sisters—the latter as lovely, devoted, and gentle, as the brothers
were bold, brave, and generous. No men were more respected by their neighbors,
or more dreaded by the Indians. At an early age, Samuel, the second son, distinguished himself as a bold and efficient borderer. As an "Indian hunter" he
had few superiors. He seemed to track the wily red man with a sagacity as remarkable as his efforts were successful. He was almost constantly engaged in
excursions against the enemy, or "scouting" for the security of the settlements.
It was mainly to these energetic operations that the frontier was so often saved
from savage depredation; and by cutting off their retreat, attacking their hunting camps, and annoying them in various other ways, he rendered himself so great
an object of fear and hatred. For these they marked him, and vowed sleepless
vengeance against the name.

During one of the many attacks and raids made by the Indians, McCulloch
was foremost. At one time, at the head of forty mounted men from Short
Creek, he made his appearance in front of the fort, the gates of which were joy-
fully thrown open. Simultaneously with the appearance of McCulloch's men
reappeared the enemy; and a rush was made, to cut off the entrance of some of
the party. All, however, succeeded in getting in except the gallant major, who,
anxious for the safety of his men, held back until his own chance was entirely
cut off. Finding himself surrounded by savages, he rode at full speed in the direction of the lofty hill which overhangs the present city of Wheeling. The enemy,
with exulting yells, followed close in pursuit, not doubting but that they would
capture one, whom of all other men, they preferred to wreak their vengeance
upon. Knowing their relentless hostility toward himself, he strained every
muscle of his noble steed to gain the summit, and then escape along the brow in
the direction of Van Metre's Fort. At length he attained the top, and galloping
ahead of his pursuers, rejoiced at his lucky escape. As he gained a point on
the hill, near where the Cumberland Road now crosses, what should he suddenly encounter but a considerable body of Indians, who were just returning from

a plundering excursion among the settlements. In an instant he comprehended the full extent of his danger. Escape seemed out of the question, either in the direction of Short Creek or back to the bottom. A fierce and revengeful foe completely hemmed him in, cutting off every chance of successful retreat or escape. What was to be done? Fall into their hands, and share the most refined torture savage ingenuity could invent? That thought was agony; and, in an instant, the bold soldier—preferring death among the rocks and brambles, to the knife and faggot of the savage—determined to plunge over the precipice before him. The hill at this point is full three hundred feet in height, and, at that time, was in many places perpendicular. Since then the construction of the road has somewhat changed its features. The exact spot where the rider went over is close to a small house standing near where the road crosses. Without a moment's hesitation, for the savages were pressing upon him, he firmly adjusted himself in his saddle, grasped securely the bridle with his left hand, and supporting his rifle in his right, pushed his unfaltering old horse over. A plunge, a crash—crackling timber and tumbling rocks were all that the wondering savages could see or hear. They looked chagrined, but bewildered, one at another; and while they inwardly regretted that the fire had been spared its duty, they could not but greatly rejoice that their most inveterate enemy was at length beyond the power of doing further injury. But lo! ere a single savage had recovered from his amazement, what should they see but the invulnerable major, on his white steed, galloping across the peninsula. Such was the feat of Major McCulloch, certainly one of the most daring and successful ever attempted. The place has become memorable as McCulloch's Leap, and will remain so as long as the hill stands, and the recollections of the past have a place in the hearts of the people.

A BOY'S BRAVERY.

The following account, taken from a communication of Major Nye, of Ohio, well illustrates of what character were the boys of the great heroic age of the west. The scene of adventure was within the present limits of Wood County, Virginia:

"I have heard from Mr. Guthrie and others, that at Bellville a man had a son, quite a youth, say twelve or fourteen years of age, who had been used to firing his father's gun, as most boys did in those days. He heard turkeys, he supposed, on or near the bank of the Ohio, opposite that place, and asked his father to let him take the gun and kill one. His father knowing that the Indians frequently decoyed people by such noises, refused, saying it was probably an Indian. When he had gone to work, the boy took the gun and paddled his canoe over the river, but had the precaution to land some distance from where he had heard the turkey all the morning, probably for fear of scaring the game, and perhaps a little afraid of Indians. The banks were steep, and the boy cautiously advanced to where he could see without being seen. Watching awhile for game, he happened to see an Indian cautiously looking over a log, to notice where the boy had landed. The lad fixed his gun at a rest, watching the place where he had seen the Indian's head, and when it appeared again, fired, and the Indian disappeared. The boy dropped the gun and ran for his canoe, which he paddled over the river as soon as possible. When he reached home, he said, 'Mother, I have killed an Indian!' 'No, you have not.' 'Yes I have,' said the boy. The father coming in, he made the same report to him, and received the same reply; but he constantly affirmed it was even so. As the gun was left, a party took the boy over the river to find it, and see the place where he shot the Indian, and, behold, his words were found verified. The ball had entered the head, where the boy had affirmed he shot, between the eye and the ear." Such boys made the men of the republic in after years—men whom neither tyranny nor oppression could subdue.

MISS MARIA M. C. HALL.

This noble woman had admiringly read of Florence Nightingale, and the noble work she did in the Crimean war; and, in the enthusiasm of a spirit naturally strong, and capable of intense devotion to an object large enough to call out all its powers, she planned for herself a course of action, and a career of usefulness, that would in effect be reproducing the Crimean heroine under our flag, and in the hospitals of our great civil conflict. From the summer of 1861 till the summer of 1865—four long, stern years—Miss Hall thought of nothing, and cared for nothing, but how she could be most useful to the suffering defenders of the national union. No patriot who shouldered his musket at the successive calls of our president felt himself more thoroughly committed to the cause, or was more determined to march and fight so long as marching and fighting remained to be done. To her with as great force as to any who thus devoted themselves to lives of loyal charity, can be applied the words which an old English author has written of woman in general: "To the honor, to the eternal honor of the sex be it recorded, that in the path of duty no sacrifice is to them too high or too dear. Nothing is with them impossible but to shrink from love, honor, innocence, and religion. The voice of pleasure or of power may pass by unheeded; but the voice of affliction, never!" Her first ambitions were checked, as she was young, cultivated, and enthusiastic, and those in authority considered this a disadvantage, as all that was required was that army nurses should be simply kind-hearted and efficient. But she was resolute in her intentions. Immediately after the battle of Antietam Creek was fought, she received a telegram from Mrs. Harris, "Meet me at McClellan's headquarters." She at once hurried to the front, finding much difficulty, unattended as she was, in penetrating the lines, and was unsuccessful in reaching the commanding general or her friend and fellow-laborer. As night was closing over the confused and bloody field, she found herself at a hospital where most of the wounded were confederates, whom the rude fortunes of war had thrown helpless upon the hands of the federal surgeons. The surgeon in charge, who very much needed assistance, begged Miss Hall to remain and aid him. This she was reluctant to do, both on account of her desire to find Mrs. Harris, and because she preferred to work for the loyal sufferers. Both these objections were soon overcome, and she entered upon her work. Her example and Christian fortitude had beneficial influences upon her protegee, and she was the means of doing much good, both directly and indirectly.

MRS. A. H. HOGE.

As among the men who enlisted in the war there was every grade of natural ability, so with the women, who, in their way enlisted also as hospital nurses and sanitary laborers, every rank in life, and all stations in society, sent their representatives into the field. The number of those who brought to the altar of their country rare gifts, and all the qualities that combine to make a woman widely known was not large. Of such, however, was Mrs. Hoge. Her first act was freely and promptly to give up her sons to the service. Together with other patriotic ladies, different fairs were held for the purpose of raising funds toward the sanitary well-being of the Union armies. The fair at Chicago had proposed twenty-five thousand dollars; it realized eighty thousand. From other similar undertakings not less than ten millions of dollars were raised and contributed to this object. Everywhere she went she was a blessing. Soldiers were cheered and prepared for trying ordeals; they were cared for and soothed by her heroic labors. All through the war Mrs. Hoge was known far and wide as a public benefactor, and the blessings showered upon her by the boys in blue, as well as those in gray, for whom she ministered, attested the sincerity of her work and purpose. She was in all respects a true type of an American woman. Virtues and traits of character centered in her that make her remembrance pleasant to contemplate for the greatness of character shown.

MRS. CHANNING.

Shortly after the commencement of the war, the family of Dr. Channing, then residing in England, removed to France, and sailed in a stout and well-armed vessel for America. They had proceeded but a little way when they were attacked by a privateer. A fierce engagement ensued, during which Mrs. Channing kept the deck, handing cartridges, aiding the wounded, and exhorting the crew to resist until death.' Their fortitude, however, did not correspond with the ardor of her wishes, and the colors were struck. Seizing the pistols and side arms of her husband, she threw them into the sea, declaring that she would rather die than see him surrender them to the enemy.

ANNA ETHERIDGE.

Were our government to order a gold medal to be given to the woman who has most distinguished herself by heroic courage in the field, and by the most patient and effective service in the military hospitals, there can be little doubt that the united voices of the soldiers and of all the army nurses would assign the honor to Anna Etheridge, of Michigan. In our "gentle Anna" was combined that true heroism which is the highest boast of manhood, with the modesty, the quiet bearing, the deferential manners and unobtrusive worth which are the loveliest traits of the fairer and the weaker sex. When the first enlistments took place, in the summer of 1861, Anna Etheridge was in Detroit, on a visit to friends. There she enlisted in the Second Michigan volunteers, under Colonel Richardson. Nineteen young ladies are said to have offered their services in the capacity of nurses, but in a few months' service every one but Anna had returned home, or lost her health, or been discharged. She was furnished with a horse, side-saddle, saddle-bags, etc., and during a battle would often ride fearlessly to the front, and whenever she found a soldier too badly hurt to go to the rear, she would dismount, and regardless of the shot and shell, produce her lint and bandages, bind up his wounds, give water or stimulating drink, then gallop on in search of another sufferer. General Berry, who for a long time commanded the brigade to which her regiment was attached, and who was remarkable for his personal gallantry in all these engagements, declares that she has remained cool and self-possessed under as hot a fire as he ever saw or was exposed to himself. At the nightly bivouac she wrapped herself in her blanket and slept on' the ground with the hardihood of a true soldier. Generally, during an engagement, she would remain a little in the rear with the surgeon, but often when she saw a man fall she would dash forward into the hottest of the fire, lift him on her horse and bring him safely to the rear, where he could have prompt attention. Many times she received balls through her dress, but was never hit. More than once when the troops showed signs of retreating she rushed to the front, seized the colors, and rallied them to a charge, shaming many into doing their duty. Though on the battle-field she seemed to be possessed and actuated by the single desire of saving the lives of the wounded men, she seldom spoke of herself, or referred to anything she had done. With the soldiers, though sharing all their hardships, she never spoke familiarly, and was held by them in the highest veneration and esteem as an angel of mercy. When general orders excluded her temporarily from the front lines, she engaged promptly in any hospital labors where aid was needed. No one of the noble women who have distinguished themselves during the war can furnish so rich, varied and romantic a series of recollections as Anna Etheridge.

MARY WASHINGTON.

As flow the crystal waters of a hallowed well-spring, glided the life of Mary Washington, thus serene, and pure, and secluded, thus genial and beneficent and blessed! It is to be lamented that no records of the youth or early womanhood of this illustrious lady have been preserved. Her husband died when George was about twelve years of age. Upon her devolved the care and guidance of the household and little flock. Order, regularity and occupation reigned supreme in her little world of home. She exacted implicit obedience from her children, and she tempered maternal tenderness with strict discipline. Mrs. Washington displayed farsight and executive ability far beyond her sex. She always counseled her son to avoid responsibilities that existing and uncontrollable circumstances might easily render not only devoid of honor or advantage, but personally unfortunate or injurious. Ever possessed of far too much genuine self-respect and enlightenment to regard the necessity of homely toil as degrading or unfortunate, her practical ingenuity and personal efforts now supplied, in a good degree, the many deficiencies and deprivations arising from the pressing exigencies of the times, and materially assisted, not only in providing for the wants of her own household, but in furnishing the means of that liberal charity which she had always exercised, notwithstanding her limited resources, and which was not remitted when increasing occasion had arisen for its continuance. When her son-in-law, Colonel Lewis, proposed to her to assume the general superintendence of her affairs, she resolutely answered: "Do you, Fielding, keep my books in order, for your eyesight is better than mine, but leave the executive management to me." Previous to his departure for France, after the termination of the Revolutionary war, the Marquis de Lafayette visited Fredericksburg expressly for the purpose of making his personal adieus to the mother of his beloved hero-friend, and that he might solemnly invoke her blessing. As the marquis, in company with one of the lady's grandsons, approached the house, he observed an aged lady working in the adjoining garden. The materials composing her dress were of home manufacture, and she wore over her time-silvered hair a plain straw bonnet. "There, sir," said the younger gentleman, "is my grandmother." Mrs. Washington received her distinguished guest with great cordiality and with her usual frank simplicity of address. "Ah, Marquis!" she exclaimed, "you see an old woman; but come, I can make you welcome to my poor dwelling without the parade of changing my dress." With unaffected piety she referred each and every occurrence in life to the great First Cause, and when the notes of jubilant praise swelled high, ever above the din of battle and the wailings of a nation's despair, it was her earnest maternal aspiration that the good boy "of her early care might never *forget himself.*" It was Mrs. Washington's habit, during the latter years of her life, to repair daily to a secluded spot near her dwelling, formed by overhanging rocks and trees. There, isolated from worldly thoughts and objects, she sought in devout prayer and meditation most appropriate preparation for the great change which she was admonished by her advanced age might nearly await her. The name of this woman will be revered and her memory cherished when those of mighty empires and world-renowned sovereigns shall have sunk forever into the whirlpool of oblivion; unsullied, unobscured by the supremacy of power and the lapse of ages, they will beam forth resplendant in the sanctified lustre of moral grandeur. She was a Christian matron, and radiant in the zenith of Columbia's heaven beams the star of her fame, fixed and enduring as

> " The cerulean arch we see,
> Majestic in its own simplicity !"

MARTHA WASHINGTON.

The reflected glory of Washington's character gave distinction to all who were connected with him by domestic ties or the bonds of consanguinity. There were many matrons of his day equally noble and virtuous as she who bore him, yet "Mary, the mother of Washington," appears the most illustrious of them all. Beauty, accomplishments and noble worth belonged to Martha Dandridge as a maiden, and Martha Custis as a wife and mother, but her crowning glory in the world's esteem is the fact that she was the bosom companion of the Father of his Country. Miss Dandridge possessed only such artificial accomplishments as the system of domestic instruction enabled her to acquire. She was, happily, endowed for usefulness and happiness by nature. Self-respect, good sense, and a quick perception of propriety were characteristics. She submitted with the utmost patience to personal privation and hardship, and did the honors of her homely camp abode with all the grace and urbanity that distinguished the mistress of the White House and of Mount Vernon. Her unwavering religious faith and her perpetual serenity and good humor not only contributed materially to the general good, but were of great service to her husband individually. Lady Washington's time and attention during each of the many seasons of her residence with the army—apart from the dearer duties and obligations arising out of her reunions with her husband—were chiefly devoted to the humane purpose of benefiting and relieving the suffering soldiers. She visited the sick, ministered to their wants, and poured that sympathy which is the "oil of joy" into their desponding hearts. She is described by those who witnessed and partook of her efforts, as having been unwavering in her zeal and earnestness in this her noble and womanly purpose. No danger delayed, no difficulty or hardship prevented the fulfillment of these benevolent duties. It is recorded of this devout Christian that never during her life, whether in prosperity or in adversity, did she omit that daily self-communion and self-examination and those private devotional exercises which would best prepare her for the self-control and self-denial by which she was, for more than half a century, so eminently distinguished. It was her habit to retire to her own apartment every morning after breakfast, there to devote an hour to solitary prayer and meditation. While her husband was President of the United States, Mrs. Washington presided with dignity over the executive mansion, both in New York and Philadelphia; but the quiet of domestic life had more charms for her than the pomp of place, and she rejoiced greatly when both sat down again, at Mount Vernon, to enjoy the repose which declining age coveted. But that pleasant dream of life soon vanished, for her companion was taken away by death a little more than two years afterward. When she was certified of the departure of his spirit, she said, "'Tis well; all is now over; I shall soon follow him; I have no more trials to pass through." In less than thirty months afterward the stricken widow was laid in the tomb, at the age of almost seventy-one years. In marble sarcophagus their remains now lie together at Mount Vernon—that Mecca of many pilgrims.

HEROISM OF THE MISSES TAYLOR.

When the North was arrayed against the South, Danville, Kentucky, was much divided in allegiance, many who had long been neighbors and friends espousing opposite causes. But there was no doubt as to the sympathies of Mrs. Taylor and her estimable family. To the breeze floated the striped bunting over her cottage, which proclaimed that their hearts and hopes and fears were all with the Union cause. When Kirby Smith occupied Danville, he sent a squad of half a dozen men to take down that piece of bunting from Mrs. Taylor's house. They were met at the door by Mrs. Taylor's two daughters, Maria and Mattie, who politely but firmly announced their intention to resist any effort to remove the national emblem. The valorous squad returned, and reported that it would require a full company to remove the flag. The force was detailed. A captain marched a hundred men with loaded guns to the door, and made a formal demand for the colors. The young ladies now came to the front door, each armed with a revolver, and holding the glorious banner between them. They replied to the confederate captain that they had vowed never to surrender that flag, and declared their intention to shoot the first one that polluted it with his touch. After hesitating a few moments the officer withdrew his force, and reported that in the exercise of his discretion he had not found it advisable to remove the colors.

MRS. RICHARD SHUBRICK.

Here was, indeed, a heroine of which to be proud. Her eyes sparkled with feeling and vivacity, while her countenance so plainly bespoke her kindness and benevolence that sorrow and misfortune instinctively sought shelter under her protection. There was an appearance of personal debility about her that rendered her peculiarly interesting; it seemed to solicit the interest of every heart, and the man would have felt himself degraded who would not put his life at hazard to serve her. Yet, when firmness of character was requisite, when fortitude was called for to repel the encroachments of aggression, there was not a more intrepid being in existence.   One noble instance only, among many, will be presented in proof. An American soldier, flying from a party of the enemy, sought her protection, which was promised.   The British pressing close upon him insisted that he should be delivered up, threatening immediate and universal destruction in case of refusal.   The ladies, her friends and companions, who were in the house with her, shrunk from the contest, and were silent, but undaunted by their threats this intrepid lady placed herself before the chamber into which the unfortunate fugitive had been conducted, and resolutely said : "To men of honor the chamber of a lady should be as sacred as a sanctuary! I will defend the passage to it, though I perish. You may succeed and enter it, but it shall be over my corpse."   "By God," said the officer, "if muskets were only placed in the hands of a few such women, our only safety would be found in retreat.   Your intrepidity, madam, gives you security; from me you shall meet no further annoyance."

NOBLE ACT OF TWO TENNESSEE WOMEN.

During the autumn, when Grant was commanding in West Tennessee in the Rebellion, with headquarters at Jackson, the twenty-seventh Iowa was ordered to take the cars at Corinth and proceed to Jackson.   It was night time and the train was crowded, men occupying the platforms, and covering the roofs of the cars.   As he approached a bridge, the engineer saw two lanterns in the distance swung to and fro with the greatest earnestness.   He gave the signal of danger, the brakes were instantly applied, the train stopped, and men sent forward to ascertain the cause of the alarm. Two women were found at the bridge, who said the coming of the loaded train of Union soldiers was known to a band of guerrillas which infested the neighborhood.   In the early part of the night the assassins had fired the bridge, and allowed the string-pieces to burn nearly off, when they extinguished the fire and left the structure standing, but so weak that it would go down as soon as a train came over it.   Hearing of this piece of dastard villiany, the women had left home in the dead of the night and traveled on foot several miles through the woods, to give an alarm and prevent the fearful consequences that would otherwise have ensued.   The officers and men whose lives were thus saved, begged of these heroic women to accept a purse of money, which was made up on the spot.   This they refused ; and all the return they would permit was that a small squad of the soldiers might see them safely home.

A BRAVE HEROINE.

In many parts of the South during the late civil struggle, the sentiment of fidelity to the Union was cherished by both sexes, with as much warmth as by any in the loyal states who volunteered their services for hospital duty, or gave up their sons and husbands to the call of patriotism. In the fall of 1862, when Bragg and Kirby Smith made their swift and inglorious retreat from Kentucky through Cumberland Gap, they were sharply pursued by Rousseau. One morning the regiment in the van—the twenty-third Kentucky—when about twenty-five miles east of Wildcat Mountain, were greatly surprised to see a squad of ragged confederates come filing slowly into camp disarmed, and a woman walking behind them with a musket in her hands. There were eleven of the confederates, and the woman handed them over to the colonel as prisoners of war. She said they came to her house the night previous, and finding that her husband was a volunteer in the Union lines, proceeded to help themselves promiscuously to everything they fancied. Some ran down the chickens, and began to kill and eat, while others cut up her carpets for horse blankets, and committed wanton depredations about the house. The incensed woman remained quiet, but watched her opportunity. Presently they were all collected in the largest room, and making merry over the fire, having left their muskets in a stack near the door. Weary, and suspecting no mischief in a solitary woman, they relaxed their watch, while she quietly removed all the fire-arms but two loaded muskets, which she took in her hands, and, standing by the door, demanded a surrender. One of them, more alert than the rest, made a spring for the muskets, but fell dead on the floor with a ball through his body. She told them quietly that any further attempt to escape would be met by a similar fate. As they had a resolute foe to deal with, discretion now became the better part of valor; they submitted to the fortunes of war, and at daylight she marched them into the Union camp as described.

ISABELLA GRAHAM.

Were the deeds of all the heroic, noble, and self-sacrificing women of the world written, they would perhaps show greater heroism and devotion than those of their brothers. "Earth hath its angels bright and lovely. They often walk in the garden of humanity unobserved. Their foot-prints are pearly with heaven's choicest blessings; fragrant flowers spring up and bloom continually in their presence, and the birds of paradise warble unceasingly in the branches beneath which they recline. They are born of true religion in the heart. Their creed comes down from heaven, and is as broad as humanity; their hope is a golden chain of promises suspended from the throne of infinite goodness; their example is a preacher of rightousness co-working with the great Redeemer."

Of such was Isabella Graham. Just before the Revolution she went with her husband to the island of Anteana. Then the furnace of affliction was prepared for her. First, intelligence came that her dear mother was buried. Soon after that two of her dear friends were removed by death; and in the autumn of 1774 her excellent husband was taken from her, after a few days illness. She afterward went to Scotland. Her aged father had become impoverished, and was added to the dependents upon her efforts for a livelihood. She opened a small school, and lived upon coarse and scanty food, made sweet by the thought that it was earned for those she loved. God prospered her, and she distributed freely of her little abundance among the more needy. A tenth of all her earnings she regularly devoted to charity; and hour after hour, when the duties of her school had ceased, that good and gentle creature would walk among the poor and destitute, in the lanes and alleys of the Scottish capital, dispensing physical benefits and religious consolations. Thoroughly purified in the crucible of sorrow, her heart was ever alive with sympathy for suffering humanity, and that became the great controlling emotion that shaped her labors. She often lent small sums of money to young persons about entering upon business, and would never receive interest, for she considered the luxury of doing good sufficient usury. She encouraged poor laboring people to unite in creating a fund for mutual relief in case of sickness, by a small deposit each week, and thus she founded the "Penny Society," out of which grew that excellent institution, in Edinburgh, "The Society for the Relief of the Destitute and Sick." Her last public labor was in forming a society for the promotion of industry among the poor. That was in the spring of 1814, when the infirmities of health and age had shortened her mission of love.

PARAGON BRAVERY.

Brave men indeed were these! In the whole range of history, and in all time, an instance of bravery more true cannot be found. It gives to us at a glance the very summit of human courage—the *ne plus ultra* of gallant intrepidity—and the rarest case of utter defiance of danger in the simple path of human duty to be found on record. After Kleber had been left by Napoleon in command of the French forces in Egypt, he sustained a number of engagements with the enemy—Turks and English—in not one of which was he defeated, and in most of which he was signally victorious, though he fought against armies from four to six and ten times more numerous than his own. In one of these battles—and one, the closing scene of which rendered it the most memorable of them all—with only two thousand men he sustained himself during five long hours of continuous fighting against the united onset of twenty thousand! At length, severely wounded himself, his little band almost entirely surrounded, and completely worn out, with only a narrow, rocky defile through which to escape, he turned his thoughts to saving the remnant of his gallant force. A retreat of the whole would simply have invited instant and total annihilation. In this extremity he saw his only hope. One of the bravest and most trustworthy officers was a chief of battalion named Chevardin. This man he summoned, and to him said : "Chevardin, if you will take a company of your grenadiers, and engage the enemy at the entrance to the ravine, I will lead our shattered army away from danger. Mark you, my dear brother; you will all be killed, but you will have saved your comrades." Said the noble chief in response, "Save the army, General. The way is open now, and it shall remain open while I have life." Then he dashed away, and quickly selected his company of grenadiers—fifty men—and frankly presented to them the situation. He said to them, in spirit, as Kleber had said to him, "You and I must offer up our lives, but our comrades we shall save to bless our memory for all time." Not a man of them hesitated, not a man quailed. Shouted a tall sergeant of grenadiers, standing bare-headed before the little band, "*Non braves*, it must be death if we remain here, sure as fate—death for all. If we can save the others, glory is ours." A quick, hearty assent was given up and down the line, and then Chevardin gave the order, " Forward !" The enemy saw the small army of the French entering the ravine, and instantly they gave the order for pursuit—" Pursue and spare not !" But at the natural outposts—a sort of rocky barbican—of the defile, they met a living wall that could not be passed. Madly, furiously, they hurled their mighty force against the martyr band, again and again until in the end the impediment had been swept away. But then it was too late, Kleber's shattered battalions had gained the safe retreat beyond the ravine, where they dared not follow.

DARING INTREPIDITY.

Kentucky, in its early days, like most new countries, was occasionally troubled by men of abandoned character, who lived by stealing the property of others, and, after committing their depredation, retired to their hiding places, thereby eluding the operation of the law. One of these marauders, a man of desperate character, who had committed extensive thefts from Mr. Samuel Daviess, as well as from his neighbors, was pursued by Daviess and a party whose property he had taken, in order to bring him to justice. While the party were in pursuit, the suspected individual, not knowing any one was pursuing him, came to the house of Daviess, armed with his gun and tomahawk—no person being at home but Mrs. Daviess and her children. After he had stepped into the house, Mrs. Daviess asked him if he would drink something; and having set a bottle of whisky on the table, requested him to help himself. The fellow, not suspecting any danger, set his gun up by the door, and while drinking, Mrs. Daviess picked up his gun, and placing herself in the door, had the gun cocked and leveled upon him by the time he turned around, and in a peremptory manner ordered him to take a seat, or she would shoot him. Struck with terror and alarm, he asked what he had done. She told him he had stolen her husband's property, and that she intended to take care of him herself. In that condition she held him a prisoner, until the party of men returned and took him into their possession.

ANN H. JUDSON.

The chapter of heroism in the field of missionary labors is as romantic as it is self-sacrificing. Ann H. Judson had been a gay young lady previous to her marriage, after which she accompanied her husband to India. When the war between the Burmese and the British government of Bengal broke out, they were in Aou, the capital of Bengal, where they had just completed preparations for missionary work. Mr. Judson was seized, cruelly treated, and kept a prisoner by the Burmese government for more than eighteen months, half of the time in triple fetters, and two months in five pair. The labors of Mrs. Judson during that time form one of the most wonderful chapters in the record of female heroism. Day after day she made intercessions before government officers for the liberation of her husband and other prisoners, but to no purpose; and every day she walked two miles to carry them food prepared with her own hands. Without her ministrations they must have perished. She had readily learned the language; and finally her appeals, written in elegant Burmese, were given to the emperor, when no officer dared mention the subject to him. The sagacious monarch, trembling for the fate of his kingdom—for a victorious English army was marching toward his capital—saw safety in employing her, and he appointed her his embassadress to General Sir Archibald Campbell, the British leader, to prepare the way for a treaty. She was received by the British commander with all the ceremony of an envoy extraordinary. She managed the affairs of the emperor with perfect fidelity, and a treaty was made through her influence, for which the proud monarch gave her great praise. She secured the release of her husband and his fellow-prisoners, and they all recommenced their missionary work. When the intense excitement which she had so long experienced was over, Mrs. Judson felt the reaction with terrible force. This, added to her great sufferings, prostrated her strength, and in the course of a few months, while Mr. Judson was absent at another post of duty, that noble disciple of Jesus fell asleep and entered upon her blessed rest.

THE HEROINES OF BRYANT'S STATION.

The brave example cannot perish
Of courage.   HOSMER.

At the siege of Bryant's Station, near Lexington, Kentucky, in August, 1782, the water in the fort was exhausted; and as the nearest place to obtain a supply was a spring several rods off, it would require no small risk, and, consequently, no common intrepidity to undertake to bring it. A body of Indians in plain sight were trying to entice the soldiers to attack them without the walls, while another party was concealed near the spring, waiting, it was supposed, to storm one of the gates, should the beseiged venture out. It was thought probable that the Indians in ambush would remain so until they saw indications that the other party had succeeded in enticing the soldiers to open engagement. The position of things was explained to the women, and they were invited to each take a bucket and march to the spring in a body. "Some, as was natural, had no relish for the undertaking, and asked why the men could not bring the water as well as themselves, observing that they were not bullet proof, and the Indians made no distinction between male and female scalps. To this it was answered that the women were in the habit of bringing water every morning to the fort; and that if the Indians saw them engaged as usual, it would induce them to think that their ambuscade was undiscovered; and that they would not unmask themselves for the sake of firing at a few women, when they hoped, by remaining concealed a few moments longer, to obtain complete possession of the fort; that if men should go down to the spring, the Indians would immediately suspect something was wrong, would despair of succeeding by ambuscade, and would instantly rush upon them, follow them into the fort, or shoot them down at the spring. The decision was soon made. A few of the boldest de-

\

clared their readiness to brave the danger, and the younger and more timid rallying in the rear of these veterans, they all marched down in a body to the spring,
within point blank shot of more than five hundred Indian warriors. Some of
the girls could not help betraying symptoms of terror; but the married women,
in general, moved with a steadiness and composure that completely deceived the
Indians. Not a shot was fired. The party were permitted to fill their buckets,
one after another without interruption; and although their steps became quicker and quicker, on their return, and when near the fort degenerated into a
rather unmilitary celerity, with some little crowding in passing the gate, yet not
more than one fifth of the water was spilled, and the eyes of the youngest had
not dilated to more than double their ordinary size."

___

"I CAN FIGHT WITH MY RIGHT HAND."

During the rebellion the sacrifices made for right were of the most sublime
character. Incidents are numerous of sterling bravery, even when the hero
was suffering, bleeding, and sometimes dying. During that awful month of June,
1862, the strife went on. Day after day the wounded were carried to the rear;
and hundreds, with shattered arms and slight flesh wounds came in on foot. A
rebel war clerk, writing of these scenes, mentions seeing a boy not more than
fifteen years old, from South Carolina, with his arm in a sling. Showing his
wound, the clerk found that a ball had entered between the fingers of his left
hand and lodged near the wrist, where the flesh was very much swollen. The
boy said, smiling, "I'm going to the hospital just to have the ball cut out, and
will then return to the battle field. I can fight with my right hand." Even
though fighting for a cause that failed, yet his bravery was of the highest order,
and his determination to aid his countrymen was commendable. Such boys always win, and advance the cause for which they fight.

___

STEPHEN GIRARD.

It is honorable to be wealthy, when wealth is honorably acquired, and when
it is used for laudable or noble purposes. After living a peaceful, happy, and
successful life, Stephen Girard died, leaving behind a fortune of about nine
millions of dollars, a very small portion of which was bequeathed to his relatives. The city of Philadelphia, in trust, was his chief legatee. He left two
millions of dollars, "or more if necessary," to build and endow a college for the
education and maintenance of "poor male orphan children," to be "received
between the ages of six and ten, and to be bound out between the ages of fourteen and eighteen, to suitable occupations, as those of agriculture, navigation,
arts, mechanical trades and manufactures." Girard was a true philanthropist.
He loved to aid and succor the poor, alleviate distress, and provide for
helpless hostages. Stephen Girard's name will ever be associated with philanthropy; and to aid others as he did is to leave behind the richest legacy to
perpetuate his memory.

A TOUCHING INCIDENT OF BRAVERY.

When President Polk issued the famous manifesto, that Mexico had "invaded our territory, and shed the blood of our fellow-citizens on our own soil," and called for volunteers to oppose the wrongs, an outburst of patriotic fervor swept over the country. In the battle of Monterey, which was occasioned by this announcement, a touching incident of bravery is recorded. A correspondent of the Louisville Courier wrote as follows concerning the incident:

"In the midst of the conflict a Mexican woman was busily engaged in carrying bread and water to the wounded men of both armies. I saw the ministering angel raise the head of a wounded man, give him water and food, and then bind up the ghastly wound with a handkerchief she took from her own head. After

A SCENE AT MONTEREY.

having exhausted her supplies, she went back to her house to get more bread and water for others. As she was returning on her mission of mercy, to comfort others, I heard the report of a gun, and the poor innocent creature fell dead. I think it was an accidental shot that struck her; I would not be willing to believe otherwise. It made me sick at heart; and, turning away from the scene, I involuntarily raised my eyes toward heaven, and thought, 'Great God! Is this war?' Passing the spot the next day, I saw her body still lying there, with the bread by her side, and the broken gourd with a few drops of water in it—emblems of her errand. We buried her; and while digging her grave, cannon balls flew around us like hail."

RICHARD M. JOHNSON.

Before our subject was twenty years of age the foundation of his future popularity and fame was laid, and his patriotism and military genius were developed by circumstances which seemed to menace the peace then existing between the United States and its Spanish neighbors in Louisiana. Negotiations finally induced the Spanish to again open the port at New Orleans to the United States vessels, and Johnson's military ardor was allowed to cool. Under command of General Harrison, he was the chief actor in the sanguinary battle on the Thames, in Canada West, in October, 1813, when the Americans gained such a decisive victory over the combined forces of British regulars, under Proctor and fifteen hundred Indians, under the renowned Tecumseh, that it ended the war in the West. Colonel Johnson led the division against the Indians, and he was in the thickest of the fight during the whole contest. Even when his bridle arm was shattered, and his horse was reeling from the loss of blood, he fough on, encouraged his men, and put the Indians to flight. When he was borne from the field, there were twenty-five bullet-holes in his person, his clothing, and his horse. He was taken to Detroit, and from thence was borne home, in great pain. In February following, though not able to walk, he took his seat in Congress. He was everywhere greeted by the people with the wildest enthusiasm as the Hero of the West. Colonel Johnson was the author of the laws which abolished imprisonment for debt in Kentucky, and of the famous report in Congress against 'the discontinuance of the mail on Sunday. He is greatly revered for his unwearied efforts in behalf of the soldiers of the Revolution and of the war of 1812 who asked Congress for pensions or relief.

BRAVERY AT ALL HAZARDS.

Such an intrepid spirit as Dicey Langston, our present heroine, possessed, was highly serviceable in the stirring times of the Revolution. Learning one time that a band of loyalists—known in those parts as the "bloody scouts"—were about to fall upon the "Elder settlement," a place where a brother of hers and other friends were residing, she resolved to warn them of their danger. To do this she must hazard her own life. But off she started, alone, in the darkness of the night. She traveled several miles through the woods, and over marshes and across creeks, through a country where foot-logs and bridges were unknown; coming to the Tyger, a rapid and deep stream, she plunged in and waded till the water was up to her neck; she then became bewildered, and zigzagged the channel for some time; reaching the opposite shore at length—for a helping hand was beneath, a kind providence guiding her—she hastened on; reached the settlement, and her brother and the whole community were safe.

She was returning one day from another settlement of whigs—in the Spartanburg district—when a company of tories met her and questioned her in regard to the neighborhood she had just left; but she refused to communicate the desired information. The leader of the band then held a pistol at her breast, and threatened to shoot her if she did not make the wished for disclosure. "Shoot me if you dare! I will not tell you!" was her dauntless reply, as she opened a long handkerchief that covered her neck and bosom, thus manifesting her willingness to receive the contents of the pistol, if the officer insisted on disclosures or life. The dastard, enraged at her defying movement, was in the act of firing, at which moment one of the soldiers threw up the hand holding the weapon, and the cowerless heart of the girl was permitted to beat on.

ALEXANDER HAMILTON.

It has been kept in memory that on the sixth of July, 1774, when the large body of mechanics had assembled in the Fields and recommended the Boston policy of suspending trade, a young man from abroad, so small and delicate in his organization that he appeared to be much younger than perhaps he really was, took part in the debate before the crowd. They asked one another the name of the gifted stranger, who shone like a star first seen above the haze, of whose rising no one has taken note. He proved to be Alaxander Hamilton, a West Indian. His mother, while he was yet a child, had left him an orphan and poor. A father's care he seems never to have known. When a mere lad, in confessing his ambition to a friend he said, "I would willingly risk my life, though not my character, to exalt my station. I mean to prepare the way for futurity; we have seen such schemes succeed when their projectors are constant." That way he prepared by integrity of conduct, diligence and study. Trained from childhood to take care of himself, he possessed a manly relf-reliance.

A REMARKABLE WOMAN.

The Wesley brothers, John and Charles, who founded Methodism, derive their greatness, like many eminent men, from their mother. She was an extraordinary woman, gifted with great intelligence and force of character. The father was eccentric and wayward, and liable to strange impulses; but the mother was calm in temperament, uniform in her methods, and of inflexible purpose. She ruled in her home, and the children learned from the cradle to yield to her unquestioning obedience. The quiet of the house was a mystery to her neighbors, for nineteen children—thirteen were living at one time—are apt to make a riot in any household. But visitors often said you would not have known there was a child in the family. She did not allow them to cry in infancy, or to romp in the house when older. She was their teacher, beginning their instruction when they were five years of age, by making them learn the alphabet in a single day. Then they were put to spelling and reading one line, then a verse, never leaving it till it was known perfectly. Their progress was very rapid under wise guidance. But though the family government was so rigid, it was administered with love, and they had the reputation of being the most loving family in the county of Lincoln.

AN ACT OF TRUE HEROISM.

When the steamer Cyprian was wrecked on the coast of Wales, the hundreds of people who stood horror stricken along the shore witnessed an act of heroism remarkable under any circumstances. The captain, John A. Strachan, of Liverpool, had told those on board that every one must look out for himself. Most of the crew had dropped overboard, and Captain Strachan also prepared to up into the billows. He tied a life-belt about his waist and mounted the rail. At that moment he noticed the pale face of a boy peering from the decks below. The lad had been an unworthy and troublesome passenger. A few hours before he was regarded as a sneak—a miserable pilferer of privileges; out now skipper only remembered he was a human being, to be saved if possible at any rate not to be left behind. Without a word Captain Strachan unbuckled the life-belt from his waist and lashed it ship-shape upon the helpless boy, bidding him save himself. "I can swim," said the captain; "take the belt." Over the side he went, lifted upon the surf like a cork; over the side went the captain, trusting, like the good, brave fellow that he was, to his strength, enfeebled with watching and anxiety. But swimming was impossible in such a sea. The boatswain, struggling for his own life, caught at the captain, who was still making headway, and both went down, never to be seen again; while the little fellow, with the good captain's life-belt about his waist, was flung upon the Welsh coast, battered about, but alive to tell the story of his strange fate and his kind friend's heroism. Such sterling heroism in the face of certain death will long serve to keep the memory of this brave captain green. He went down for another. This is the truest test of great magnanimity.

THE BENEVOLENT COUNTESS.

A noble lady of England, the Countess Ebersburg, is engaged in a philanthropic work, for which she was prepared by the death of two babes of her own, and she then consecrated her fortune and life to the single work of saving the lives of children. As she began to examine the subject, she met with the statement that in England two hundred thousand children die annually under the age of five, and of these three per cent. die of preventable causes. Then she set herself to the task of going around and visiting the poor, and conversing with mothers. In the first place, she instituted weekly mothers' meetings, which might be attended by those who were able, at which she gave them instructions in economizing their poor means, and in the kinds of food most nourishing, and answered from the best authorities the mothers' questions as to treating their own and their children's ailments. The countess next drew upon her own means and those of her friends to provide malted-food extract and similar things for ailing children, and by spending about £400 a year in this way saved many lives. The ill-spelt, tear-blotted letters of gratitude showered upon her by grateful mothers are preserved by her as proudly as any warrior preserves the medals that reward his successful slaughters. No cry of mother or child has ever been

unheeded. Gradually she has extended her plans to include a children's retreat
in the country, for babies whose lives depend upon a change of air, and a day
nursery, where women may leave their children in good care while they are at
work. Her work is now arranged in districts amid the poorest parts of London,
and she distributes some nine thousand pounds o. baby food per annum. Instructions as to health are given in four different centers. A great many ealets
containing simple sanitary instructions are also distributed.

BRAVERY OF MRS. HENDEE.

On the burning of Royalton, Vermont, by the Indians, in 1776, Mrs. Hendee,
of that place, exhibited a praiseworthy and heroic character. The attack was
sudden, and her husband being absent in the Vermont regiment, and she being
in the field, the Indians seized her children, carried them across White River, at
that place perhaps a hundred yards wide and quite deep for fording, and placed
them under the keepers having the other persons they had collected—thirty or
forty in number—in charge. On discovering the fate of her children Mrs.
Hendee resolutely dashed into the river, waded through, and fearlessly entering
the Indian camp, regardless of their tomahawks menacingly flourished around
her head, boldly demanded the release of her little ones, and persevered in her
alternate upbraidings and supplications till her request was granted. She then
carried her children back through the river and landed them in safety on the
other bank. But not content with what she had done, like a patriot as she was,
she immediately returned, begged for the release of the children of others, again
was rewarded with success, and brought two or three more away; again returned
and again succeeded, till she had rescued the whole fifteen of her neighbors'
children who had been thus snatched away from their parents. On her last return to the camp of the enemy, the Indians were so struck with her conduct
that one of them declared that so brave a squaw deserved to be carried across
the river, and offered to take her on his back and carry her over. She in the
same spirit accepted the offer, mounted the back of the savage, and was carried
to the opposite bank, where she collected her rescued troop of children, and
hastened away to restore them to their over-joyed parents.

THE BOY HERO.

In a sermon designed to teach that a life of self-sacrifice is the only life worth
living, a New York preacher tells the following touching anecdote: A rough
teacher in a school called up a poor, half-starved lad, who had violated the laws
of the school, and said, "Take off your coat, sir!" The boy refused to take it
off. The teacher said again, "Take off your coat," as he swung the whip through
the air. The boy refused. It was not because he was afraid of the lash—he was
used to that at home—but it was from shame; he had no undergarment. And as
at the third command he pulled slowly off his coat, there went a sob all through
the school. They saw then why he did not want to remove his coat, and they

saw the shoulder blades had almost cut through the skin, and a stout, healthy boy rose up and went to the teacher of the school and said, "Oh, sir, please don't hurt this poor fellow! Whip me. He's nothing but a poor chap. Don't hurt him—he's poor. Whip me." "Well," said the teacher, "its going to be a severe whipping; I am willing to take you as a substitute." "Well," said the boy, "I don't care. You may whip me if you will let this poor fellow go." The stout, healthy boy took the scourging without an outcry. Probably not one of our readers but will say "Bravo!" But how many will not only admire but imitate the spirit of that self-sacrifice?

BRAVE SERGEANT ORD.

In every instance where this heroic soldier was engaged in action, he not only increased his own reputation, but animated those around him by his lively courage. In camp, on a march, and in every situation, he performed his duties with cheerfulness and vivacity, preserving always the most orderly conduct. At the surprise of Georgetown, being with a small party of the Legion Infantry, in possession of an inclosure, surrounding a house from which they had expelled the enemy, the recovery of the position was sought by a British force, whose leader approaching the gate of entrance, exclaimed, "Rush on, my brave fellows, they are only worthless militia, and have no bayonets!" Ord immediately placed himself in front of the gate, and as they attempted to enter, laid six of his enemies, in succession, dead at his feet, crying out at every thrust, "No bayonets here—none at all, to be sure!" following up his strokes with such rapidity that the British party could make no impression, and were compelled to retire.

AN UNDOUBTED HEROINE.

Among the most harrowing disasters that daily occur are those of the sea. Our present heroine has all her life been of great service to vessels that flounder about Fairweather Island, located sixty miles north of the city of New York. The island is about half a mile from shore, and contains five acres of land. On that little, secluded spot Captain Moore has resided nearly a quarter of a century, and has reared a family of five children, of whom Kate is the heroine. Disasters frequently occur to vessels which are driven around Montauk Point, and sometimes in the sound, when they are homeward bound; and at such times she is always on the alert. She has so thoroughly cultivated the sense of hearing that she can distinguish amid the howling storm the shrieks of the drowning mariners, and thus direct a boat, which she has learned to manage most dexterously, in the darkest night, to the spot where a fellow mortal is perishing. Though well educated and refined, she possesses none of the affected delicacy which characterizes too many town-bred misses; but, adapting herself to the peculiar exigencies of her father's humble yet honorable calling, she is ever ready to lend a helping hand, and shrinks from no danger if duty points that way. In the gloom and terror of the stormy night, amid perils at all hours of the day and all seasons of

the year, she has launched her barque on the threatening way   and has assisted
her aged and feeble father in saving the lives of scores of persons. Such conduct, like that of Grace Darling, to whom Kate Moore has been justly compared,
needs no comment; it stamps its moral at once and indelibly upon the heart of
every reader.

A GIRL'S COOL COURAGE.

Two of the most essential elements of true bravery are a cool head and a stout
heart. The following incident illustrates how truly courageous was the heroine:
The children of Judge Winchester were at school, and in returning home had
to cross Hickory Creek. Mr. Winchester had sent a team for them, and the
children jumping into the wagon started for home. In crossing the stream a
sudden rush of water caught the wagon, it became uncoupled, and the bed and
hind wheels started down stream in imminent danger of being capsized momenta-
rily. A daughter of Mr. Winchester's, only twelve years old, comprehending
the danger, cooly picked up each one of the little children and threw them out,
while men caught them as they splashed in the water near the edge of the banks,
After all had been rescued, she leaped from the treacherous craft and was
caught up by the willing hands on the bank, and in an instant the wagon capsized. The act was truly heroic. The horses were also saved, and the wrecked
wagon recovered from the banks of the stream below, where it drifted and
lodged.

SERGEANT WHALING.

In proportion as the soldiers of the Revolution were removed from that rank
in society in which an enlargement of ideas and expansion of mind was to be
looked for, must be their merit, who, under the exalted influences of military
and patriotic enthusiasm, evinced a nobleness of soul, and chivalric intrepidity,
increasing their own fame, and giving a higher stamp of celebrity to the American character. What can be said of the soldiers in general can be said of Sergeant Whaling with emphasis. When the importance of wresting the possession
of Stockade Fort, at Ninety-Six, from the enemy was clearly ascertained, Lieutenant-colonel Lee, to whom the charge of directing all operations against it
was intrusted by General Greene, adopted the opinion that it might be effected
by fire. Accordingly, Sergeant Whaling, a gallant non-commissioned officer,
who had served with zeal and fidelity from the commencement of the Revolution,
and whose period of enlistment would have expired in a few days, with twelve
privates, were sent forward in open day, and over level ground that afforded no
cover to facilitate their approaches, to accomplish this hazardous enterprise.
Whaling saw with certainty the death on which he was about to rush, but by the
prospect of which he was unappalled. He dressed himself neatly, took an affectionate but cheerful leave of his friends, and with his musket swung over his
shoulder, and a bundle of blazing pine torches in his hand, sprung forward for

the object of his attack. His alacrity inspired the little band with courage. They followed him closely up to the building around which the stockade was erected before the troops within fired a shot. Their aim was deliberate and deadly. But one individual escaped with his life. Whaling fell deeply lamented by all. Instead of the rash and unavailing exposure to which he was subjected, all admitted his just claim to promotion—grieved that his valuable life was not preserved for those services he had so often shown himself so capable of rendering. But by the devotion to the interests of country, and daring intrepidity, was the British lion driven from our shores, and the stars and stripes allowed to float triumphantly to the breeze. What greater honor can there be than to die for one's country?

A HERO REWARDED.

In one of the hotly-contested fights in Virginia during the war, a federal officer fell wounded in front of the confederate breastworks. While lying there wounded and crying piteously for water, a confederate soldier, James Moore, of Burke County, North Carolina, declared his intention of supplying him with drink. The bullets were flying thick from both sides, and Moore's friends endeavored to dissuade him from such a hazardous enterprise. Despite remonstrance and danger, however, Moore leaped the breastworks, canteen in hand, reached his wounded enemy and gave him a drink. The federal, under a sense of gratitude for the timely service, took out his gold watch and offered it to his benefactor, but it was refused. The officer then asked the name of the man who had braved such danger to succor him. The name was given, and Moore returned unhurt to his position behind the embankment. They saw nothing more of each other. Moore was subsequently wounded, and lost a limb in one of the engagements in Virginia, and returned to his home in Burke County. Years afterward he received a communication from the federal soldier to whom he had given the "cup of cold water" on the occasion alluded to, announcing that he had settled on him the sum of $10,000, to be paid in four annual installments, of $2,500 each. Investigation has established the fact that there is no mistake or deception in the matter.

CHARACTERISTIC REVOLUTIONARY WOMAN.

When the Revolutionary war broke out Mrs. Elizabeth Martin, one of the pioneer mothers "whose bosoms pillowed men," had seven sons old enough to enlist in their country's service, and as soon as the call to arms was heard she said to them, "Go, boys, and fight for your country; fight till death if you must, but never let your country be dishonored. Were I a man I would go with you."

Several British officers once called at her house, and while receiving some refreshments, one of them asked her how many sons she had. She told him, eight; and when asked where they were, she boldly replied, "seven of them are

4

engaged in the service of their country." The officer sneeringly observed that she had enough of them. "No, sir, I wish I had fifty!" was her prompt and proud reply. Only one of those seven sons was killed during the war. He was a captain of artillery, served in the sieges of Savannah and Charleston, and was slain at the siege of Augusta. Soon after his death a British officer called on the mother, and in speaking of this son, inhumanely told her that he saw his brains blown out on the battle-field. The reply she made to the monster's observation was: "He could not have died in a nobler cause." When Charleston was besieged, she had three sons in the place. She heard the report of cannon on the occasion, though nearly a hundred miles west of the city. The wives of the sons were with her, and manifested great uneasiness while listening to the reports; nor could the mother control her feelings any better. While they were indulging in silent and, as we may suppose, painful reflections, the mother suddenly broke the silence by exclaiming, as she raised her hands: "Thank God! They are the children of the republic."

BOLD ADVENTURE OF A PATRIOTIC GIRL.

At the time General Greene retreated before Lord Rawdon from Ninety-Six, when he had passed Broad River, he was very desirous to send an order to General Sumter, who was on the Wateree, to join him, that they might attack Rawdon, who had divided his force. But the general could find no man in that part of the state who was bold enough to undertake so dangerous a mission. The country to be passed through for many miles was full of blood-thirsty tories, who, on every occasion that offered, imbrued their hands in the blood of the whigs. At length Emily Geiger presented herself to General Greene, and proposed to act as his messenger; and the general, both surprised and delighted, closed with her proposal. He accordingly wrote a letter and delivered it, and at the same time communicated the contents of it verbally, to be told to Sumter in case of accident. Emily was young, but as to her person or adventures on the way we have no further information, except that she was mounted on horseback, upon a side-saddle, and on the second day of her journey she was intercepted by Lord Rawdon's scouts. Coming from the direction of Greene's army, and not being able to tell an untruth without blushing, Emily was suspected and confined to a room; and as the officer in command had the modesty not to search her at the time, he sent for an old tory matron as more fitting for that purpose. Emily was not wanting in expedient, and as soon as the door was closed and the bustle a little subsided, she *ate up the letter*, piece by piece. After a while the matron arrived, and upon searching carefully, nothing was to be found of a suspicious nature about the prisoner, and she would disclose nothing. Suspicion being thus allayed, the officer commanding the scouts suffered Emily to depart whither she said she was bound; but she took a route somewhat circuitous to avoid further detention, and soon after found the road to Sumter's camp, where she arrived in safety. Emily told her adventure, and delivered Greene's verbal message to Sumter, who, in consequence, soon after joined the main army at Orangeburgh.

HORACE GREELEY.

When Horace Greeley died, one of the brightest beacon lights in the journalistic and philantbropic firmament went out, and the diminished rays of his greatness became emblems of sadness. During all of his singularly upright and honorable career, there was ever the same frankness of spirit and magnanimity of purposes displayed. His parents and family were in impecunious circumstances, and this fact above all others contributed in making him "a self-made man." His ancestors were of the severe Scotch-Irish descent, many of whose peculiarities were prominent in the composition of his character. After his parents had moved to Westlake, Vermont, where the father was barely able to support his family, Horace started off alone to East Poultney, a small village, determined, if possible, to obtain an apprenticeship as a printer. He was then but thirteen years of age, and even long before this immature period he had formed the settled purpose of following the "black art." Soon after, his father's family moved across the Alleghanies, and settled near Erie, Pennsylvania, where a small tract of land was purchased. Even the small amount necessary for this purchase greatly impoverished his father and laid another burden on his shoulders. During the first part of Horace's apprenticeship, he received about twenty dollars a year as compensation, besides his board. The greater part of this small sum he scrupulously saved, and sent from time to time to his father. This noble trait of character is commendable and unusual. The care of his parents was always his pleasure, and the assistance which he rendered them on the many different occasions bespeaks the nobility of his character. From the time he went single handed and alone to New York city, illy clad, and almost moneyless, until he attained the proud distinction of "founder of the Tribune," for which the world honors and remembers him to-day, until the day of his sad death, he was always honored for his honesty, application, promptness, and reliability. The character of Horace Greeley is one of which Americans can well be proud, and is a fit example for the youth of the land to study and follow. If the history of his life were told in a nut-shell, it would be, " He lived true to himself, and won the proud distinction of being the founder of one of the greatest journalistic ventures of the world."

A TINY HEROINE.

It is always pleasant to record examples of child usefulness, and even very little children are sometimes, in situations of sudden trial and need, the instruments of help and rescue. While Mrs. Woodworth was on a visit to her sister, Mrs. Smith, residing at Pelican, Minnesota, the latter, one night, was taken ill. Mr. Smith was away from home at the time, and there was no one near the house to render assistance save Mrs. Woodworth and a little three-year-old daughter of Mrs. Smith. Mrs. Woodworth could not leave, so she called little Angie and asked her to go to the house of a neighbor, three quarters of a mile distant, and summon assistance. The child did as directed in an incredibly short space of time, and upon her return with the neighbor it was found necessary to summon a physician. It was now nearly dark and a storm was brewing, yet this brave little heroine again took the road and went to the nearest neighbor's house, a distance of one and a fourth miles in the opposite direction from her first trip, where she found a man to go for a physician. Ere her return to her home the storm had so increased as to render her progress very slow, and the vivid and constant lightning might have stricken terror into the heart of many an older pedestrian; yet this three-year-old child bravely and faithfully performed her mission and returned in safety.

A BRAVE DEED.

The scout who led General Gibbon to the scene of Custer's massacre was a frontiersman, named Beidler. As soon as the remains of the slaughtered soldiers were buried, General Gibbon wanted to send a messenger to Fort Ellis. This was a terrible undertaking; the mountains literally swarmed with hostile Sioux. There were ninety-nine chances out of a hundred that the messenger would never reach his destination. To order any one to take it was like signing a death warrant, and even the brave Gibbon shrank from this. He called up a half-dozen men, and proposed to them the undertaking.

"Boys," said Gibbon, " I can't order you on this desperate hazard, for I believe in my soul it is almost certain death, and yet I must do my duty and send the message. If none of the scouts will go, I will send my nephew."

Sitting a few paces apart from the officers and men was Beidler, cleaning his gun and polishing his equipments—a stout, heavy-built man of forty years of age. As Gibbon ceased speaking, the frontiersman's voice rose clear and distinct.

"Never mind, General; I'll carry your message."

Gibbon turned toward him in surprise. "What, you, X.? Why, man, I couldn't ask you to do such a thing! Besides, you are our guide."

"Yes, I know; but I don't mind the venture. Any way, I'll carry the message."

"You know better than I do, X., that it's a deadly venture. I wouldn't have dared to ask you."

"It's all right, General. Get your letter ready and let me have it at dark."

Then rising to his feet he limped away, for X. Beidler was lame. An Indian bullet in one of the wild forays of the border had shattered his hip, and although the wound had long since healed, it had left him lame for life. Two hours later, when the shadows of a mountain twilight were falling thick and dusky over the valley, he cautiously rode down the valley of the Little Horn and disappeared from view. About the incidents of that desperate ride of four hundred miles, of his hair-breadth escapes, of his desperate adventures, it would be impossible in the limits of an article like this to give anything like an adequate description. It will suffice to say that the message was carried.

Sometime afterward when he was met by friends, he was preparing for his return trip down the Yellowstone, and seemed as careless, and talked as unconcernedly about his exploit as one might speak of a trip to Boonville or St. Louis, and yet he had just performed a deed which the boldest frontiersman would have shrunk from in dismay.

———

THE YOUNG HEROINE OF FORT HENRY.

The siege of Fort Henry, at the mouth of Wheeling Creek, in Ohio County, Virginia, occurred in September, 1777. Of the historical *fact* most people are aware; yet but few, comparatively, knew how much the little band in the garrison, who held out against thirty or forty times their number of savage assailants, were indebted, for their success, to the courage and self-devotion of a single female. The Indians kept up a brisk firing from about sunrise till past noon, when they ceased and retired a short distance to the foot of a hill. During the forenoon the little company in the fort had not been idle. Among their number were a few sharp-shooters, who had burnt most of the powder on hand to the best advantage. Almost every charge had taken effect, and probably the savages began to see that they were losing numbers at fearful odds, and had doubtless retired for consultation. But they had less occasion for anxiety, just at that time, than the men, women and children in the garrison. As already hinted, the stock of powder was nearly exhausted. There was a keg in a house ten or twelve rods from the gate of the fort, and as soon as the hostilities of the Indians were suspended, the question arose, Who shall attempt to seize this prize? Strange to say, every soldier proffered his services, and there was an ardent contention among them for the honor. In the weak state of the garrison, Colonel Shepard, the commander, deemed it advisable that only one person should be spared; and in the midst of the confusion, before any one could be designated, a girl named

Elizabeth Zane, interrupted the debate, saying that her life was not so important at that time as any one of the soldier's, and claiming the privilege of performing the contested service. The colonel would not at first listen to her proposal; but she was so resolute, so persevering in her plea, and her argument was so powerful, that he finally suffered the gate to be opened, and she passed out. The Indians saw her before she reached her brother's house, where the keg was deposited; but, for some unknown cause, they did not molest her, until she reappeared with the article under her arm. Probably divining the nature of her burden, they discharged a volley as she was running toward the gate; but the whizzing balls only gave agility to her feet, and herself and the prize were quickly safe within the gate. The result was that the soldiers, inspired with enthusiasm by this heroic adventure, fought with renewed courage, and, before the keg of powder was exhausted, the enemy raised the siege.

CAPTAIN RICHARD GOUGH.

The magnanimity and independence of spirit of this intrepid officer won him great esteem. On one occasion, having been a prisoner, he had been thrown into irons and treated with peculiar indignity. A change in the political occurrences of the time, highly favorable to America, having taken place, many of the adherents of Britain, repenting the imprudence of their conduct, wished, by a full confession of error, to be admitted to the rights of citizenship. An American who had interested himself very highly in favor of an individual subjected to the penalties of the confiscation law, making an appeal to the humanity of Captain Gough, said, "I am sensible that it is only necessary for you to oppose the petition in his behalf, which will be presented to the legislature, to ensure its failure." "Make yourself easy, then," was the generous reply. "Give me the petition—I will present and support it, and shall be happy if that prevents opposition from any other quarter. The war is brought to a happy conclusion—my resentments are no more." It gave additional lustre to this act of generosity that a little before, while at supper with his aged mother, he had been fired upon and desperately wounded by a Tory party from the British garrison.

A PATRIOTIC DONATION.

When General Greene was retreating through the Carolinas, after the battle of the Cowpens, and while at Salisbury, North Carolina, he put up at a hotel, the landlady of which was Mrs. Elizabeth Steele. A detachment of Americans had just had a skirmish with the British under Cornwallis' at the Catawba ford, and were defeated and dispersed, and when the wounded were brought to the hotel the general no doubt felt somewhat discouraged, for the fate of the south and perhaps of the country seemed to hang on the result of this memorable retreat. Added to his other troubles was that of being penniless, and Mrs. Steele, learning this fact by accident, and ready to do any thing in her power to further the cause of freedom, took him aside and drew from under her apron two bags of specie. Presenting them to him she generously said, "Take these, for you will want them and I can do without them." Never did relief come at a more propitious moment; nor would it be straining conjecture to suppose that he resumed his journey with his spirits cheered and brightened by this touching proof of woman's devotion to the cause of her country.

HEROIC BOY.

Calm, true courage, which does quietly what its hand findeth to do, was exhibited some years ago, by a boy on board a burning steamer on the St. Lawrence: Narcisse Lamontayne, aged thirteen years, saved eight children from the wreck. He accomplished his noble deed by seizing the door of a stateroom, placing the children upon it, and pushing it before him while he swum. By several such trips he succeeded in landing on a dry rock, or on the beach, eight of the children that were on board the ill-fated vessel. A country composed of such boys has the surest foundation for future greatness. They are the boys who make our Washingtons, our Lincolns and our Garfields.

DARING EXPLOIT OF "TWO REBELS."

During the sieges of Augusta and Cambridge, two young men of the name of Martin, belonging to Ninety-Six district, South Carolina, were in the army. Meanwhile their wives, who remained at home with their mother-in-law, displayed as much courage, on a certain occasion, as was exhibited, perhaps, by any female during the struggle for independence. Receiving intelligence one evening that a courier, under guard of two British officers, would pass their house that night with important dispatches, Grace and Rachel Martin resolved to surprise the party and obtain the papers. Disguising themselves in their husbands' outer garments and providing themselves with arms, they waylaid the enemy. Soon after they took their station by the roadside the courier and his escort made their appearance. At the proper moment the disguised ladies sprang from their bushy covert, and presenting their pistols, ordered the party to surrender their papers. Surprised and alarmed, they obeyed without hesitation or the least resistance. The brave women having put them on parole, hastened home by the nearest route, which was a by-path through the woods, and dispatched the documents to General Greene by a single messenger, who probably had more courage than the trio that lately bore them. Strange to say, a few minutes after the ladies reached home, and just as they had doffed their male attire, the officers, retracing their steps, rode up to the house and craved accommodations for the night. The mother of the heroines asked them the cause of their so speedy return after passing her house, when they exhibited their paroles and said that "two rebels" had taken them prisoners. Here the young ladies, in a rallying mood, asked them if they had no arms, to which query they replied, that, although they had, they were arrested so suddenly that they had no time to use them. We have only to add that they were hospitably entertained, and the next morning took their leave of the women as ignorant of the residence of their captors as when first arrested.

A RARE PROOF OF DEVOTION.

Not long since F. A. Learett, of Oakland, an engineer in the employ of the Central Pacific Railroad Company, and stationed in Arizona, was seriously scalded by the overturning of his locomotive, and one of his legs was so badly injured that the flesh fell away. The attending physicians told him that if his friends would each contribute a small piece of flesh they could repair the limb and restore it to its old usefulness. The statement was widely circulated, and twenty-eight of his fellow-workmen volunteered and bravely bared their limbs to the surgeon's knife. The transplantation of flesh was successfully made and to-day the leg looks almost as natural as does the uninjured member. The heroic act of the men was duly rewarded. The railroad company hearing of the case, leave of absence was given and two months' extra pay was ordered paid to each of the men.

A KENTUCKY AMAZON.

During the summer of 1787, the house of Mr. John Merril, of Nelson county, Kentucky, was attacked by the Indians, and defended with singular address and good fortune. Merril was alarmed by the barking of a dog about midnight, and upon opening the door in order to ascertain the cause of the disturbance, he received the fire of six or seven Indians, by which his arm and thigh were both broken. He instantly sank upon the floor and called upon his wife to close the door. This had scarcely been done when it was violently assailed by the tomahawks of the enemy, and a large breach soon effected. Mrs. Merril, however, being a perfect Amazon, both in strength and courage, guarded it with an ax, and successfully killed or badly wounded four of the enemy as they attempted to force their way into the cabin. The Indians then ascended the roof and attempted to enter by way of the chimney; but here again they were met by the same determined enemy. Mrs. Merril seized the only feather bed which the cabin afforded, and hastily riping it open, poured its contents upon the fire. A furious blaze and stifling smoke instantly ascended the chimney, and brought down two of the enemy, who lay for a few moments at the mercy of the lady. Seizing the ax she quickly dispatched them, and was immediately summoned to the door, where the only remaining savage now appeared, endeavoring to effect an entrance while Mrs. Merril was engaged at the chimney. He soon received a gash in the cheek which compelled him, with a loud yell, to relinquish his purpose, and return hastily to Chillicothe, where, according to the report of a prisoner, he gave an exaggerated account of the fierceness, strength, and courage of the "long-knife squaw."

MRS. MERRIL'S BRAVE DEFENSE.—*Page 104.*

FARADAY, THE PHILOSOPHER.

The life of Michael Faraday is pre-eminently that of a Christian philosopher, and therefore honorable. It is full of beautiful lessons from its opening to its close. He was the son of very poor people, who rented two rooms over a stable in a London mews; he rose to such high position that he would have been welcomed at the tables of the noblest in the land; and yet he never showed the slightest touch of pride. He might have become very rich and very influential in worldly respect, but he chose to remain poor and to live a simple life; and he has in this respect also left us the choicest example. Scarcely had he shown his real capacity when he was assailed with requests to work commercially. At first he yielded, made analysis, and at first made money; but at length the question had to be faced and finally disposed of, whether he was to sink into a commercial analyst and in a few years become a rich man, or be a great discoverer and remain comparatively a poor one. He nobly chose the latter alternative, and consistently acted upon it till the end. Only for the state did he depart from his rule, as a good citizen, setting his own plans and schemes for a time aside, to forward the arms of the crown and so far as in him lay to secure the public good. He was thus, without doubt, one of our noblest heroes at the same time that he was the finest specimen of the experimental philosopher which England ever produced. The flowers which such a man as Faraday gladly gathered in the hope of pleasing others and benefiting them, form the best wreath that those left behind can weave and cast upon his grave.

NOBLE PHILANTHROPY.

The investigator may search over the entire field of philanthropy, he may study the lives of the noblest, and yet when he glances over the career and motives of Edward Denison, he cannot but be impressed with the fact that his life was characterized by the highest disinterested spirit of philanthropy of which history tells. Let another tell the story of his life. "One evening, not very long ago, I went down to have a look at Philpot Street; because, in the month of July, 1867, a young gentleman took it into his head to engage lodgings there, and for the greater part of the year went out and in as regularly as though he had fallen into reduced circumstances, and, compelled to catch at whatever chance first offered, in desperation, and spite a weakly constitution, had become a clerk at one of the neighboring yards or factories. He had not, however, gone to Philpot Street out of any necessity, though clearly he had chosen it as a place of residence because it occupied so central a position in the East End. The son of a bishop, with high university distinctions, and the prospect before him of a great political career, he had hardly reached manhood when he was so deeply moved by what he had heard and read of the condition of the poor, that he resolved to devote his life to the study of the question and to the amelioration of their condition. His reading and his reflections soon led him to the conclusion that there was something fatally defective in the administration of the Poor

Law, while yet indiscriminate charity was the parent of pauperism; that little was to be hoped for from emigration, which, as he conceived, for the most part only carried away the sinew from laboring population, who were all wanted at home, leaving behind the vicious residuum still to be dealt with, and that those who help the poor must devote themselves chiefly to the rising generation, and teach them the best way to help themselves. He was desirous to see with his own eyes how matters stood; to come into daily contact with the people, and learn their feelings and prejudices, to watch the doings of the guardians and others, and, if possible, to suggest practical means of meeting the great difficulty of the day. And so, turning his back for a time on Chesham Place, W. Edward Denison, then only twenty-seven years of age, " went into residence " at Philpot Street, London, to visit the hovels, to teach the children through the day and the adults at night, and to play the part generally of a volunteer poor-inspector," visiting fever-stricken streets, organizing schools, one of which he kept up entirely at his own cost, teaching the children, and lecturing to working men at nights, while, for a little relief, he read law in his spare time—this was the order of the day while Edward Denison dwelt in Philpot Street. Taking into consideration his great talents, his beautiful character, his steady affection, his capacity of self-denial, and his unwearied devotion in the cause he had taken up, the grandeur of the hero stands out in bold relief.

CORNELIA BEEKMAN.

Mrs. Cornelia Beekman was a daughter of Pierre Van Cortlandt, Lieutenant Governor of New York from 1777 to 1795; and she seems to have inherited her father's zeal for the rights of his country. She was born at the Cortlandt manor house, "an old fashioned stone mansion situated on the banks of the Croton river," in 1752; was married when about seventeen or eighteen, to General G. Beekman, and died on the 14th of march, 1847. A few anecdotes will illustrate the noble characteristics of her nature:

A party of tories, under command of Colonels Bayard and Fleming, once entered her house, and, with a great deal of impudence and in the most insulting tone, asked if she was not "the daughter of that old rebel, Pierre Van Cortlandt?" "I am the daughter of Pierre Van Cortlandt, but it becomes not such as you to call my father a rebel," was her dauntless reply. The person who put the question now raised his musket, at which menacing act she coolly reprimanded him and ordered him out of doors. His heart melted beneath the fire of her eye, and, abashed, he sneaked away.

In one instance, a man named John Webb, better known at that time as "Lieutenant Jack," left in her charge a valise which contained a new suit of uniform and some gold. He stated he would send for it when he wanted it, and gave her particular directions not to deliver it to any one without a written order from himself or his brother Samuel. About two weeks afterward, a man named Smith rode up to the door in haste, and asked her husband, who was without, for Lieutenant Jack's valise. She knew Smith, and had little confidence in his *professed* whig principles; so she stepped to the door and reminded her husband that it would be necessary for the messenger to show his order before the valise could be given.

"You know me very well, Mrs. Beekman; and when I assure you that Lieutenant Jack sent me for the valise, you will not refuse to deliver it to me, as he is greatly in want of his uniform."

"I do know you very well—*too well* to give you the valise without a written order from the owner or the colonel."

Soon after this brief colloquy, Smith went away without the valise, and it was afterward ascertained that he was a rank tory, and at that very hour in league with the British. Indeed, Major Andre was concealed in his house that day, and had Smith got possession of Webb's uniform, as the latter and Andre were about the same size, it is likely the celebrated spy would have escaped and changed the reading of a brief chapter of American history. Who can tell how much this republic is indebted to the prudence, integrity, courage and patriotism of Cornelia Beekman?

HEROISM OF SCHOHARIE WOMEN.

During the struggle for Independence there were three noted forts in the Schoharie settlement, called the Upper, Middle and Lower; and when, in the autumn of 1780, Sir John Johnson sallied forth from Niagara, with his five hundred or more British, tory and German troops, and made an attack on these forts, an opportunity was given for the display of patriotism and courage, as well by the women of the settlement as by the men. When the Middle fort was invested, an heroic and noted ranger named Murphy used his rifle balls so fast as to need an additional supply; and, anticipating his wants, Mrs. Angelica Vrooman caught his bullet mould, some lead and an iron spoon, ran to her father's tent, and there moulded a quantity of bullets amid

> "the shout
> Of battle, the barbarian yell, the bray
> Of dissonant instruments, the clang of arms,
> The shriek of agony, the groan of death."

While the firing was kept up at the Middle fort, great anxiety prevailed at the Upper; and during this time Captain Hager, who commanded the latter, gave orders that the women and children should retire to a long cellar, which he specified, should the enemy attack him. A young lady named Mary Haggidorn, on hearing these orders, went to Captain Hager and addressed him as follows: "Captain, I shall not go into that cellar. Should the enemy come, I will take a spear, which I can use as well as any *man*, and help defend the fort." The captain, seeing her determination, made the following reply: "Then take a spear, Mary, and be ready at the pickets to repel an attack." She cheerfully obeyed, and held the spear at the picket till huzzas for the American flag burst on her ear, and told that all was safe.

PATRIOTIC WOMEN OF OLD MIDDLESEX.

After the departure of Colonel Prescott's regiment of "minute-men," Mrs. David Wright, of Pepperell, Mrs. Job Shattuck, of Groton, and the neighboring women, collected at what is now Jewett's Bride, over the Nashua, between Pepperell and Groton, clothed in their absent husbands' apparel, and armed with muskets, pitchforks, and such other weapons as they could find; and having elected Mrs. Wright their commander, resolutely determined that no foe to freedom, foreign or domestic, should pass that bridge. For rumors were rife that the regulars were approaching, and frightful stories of slaughter flew rapidly from place to place and from house to house. Soon there appeared one on horseback, supposed to be treasonably engaged in conveying intelligence to the enemy. By the implicit command of Sergeant Wright he is immediately arrested, unhorsed, searched, and the treasonable correspondence found concealed in his boots. He was detained prisoner, and sent to Oliver Prescott, Esq., of Groton, and his dispatches were sent to the Committee of Safety. The annals of the Revolution furnish scores of such daring maneuvers on the part of the heroic women, and to them much of renown must be given that Independence was at last proclaimed.

WALTER POWELL, THE MAN OF BUSINESS.

The life of Walter Powell is a rich gift to us in the present day. It shows us how a man in our own day rose from a comparatively low position to wealth and influence, and how he won the love and esteem of all who knew him, sheerly by the beauty of his Christian character and the elevated consistency of his life. Our young men need to be brought under the savor of such a bright example. His life was not remote or distant; he was tried as they are likely to be, and yet by grace he was sustained and strengthened. His memoir gives the clearest testimony that the best man of business may also be the truest of Christians, that there is no necessary opposition between them, that strict justice and high principle are the best assurances of success, and that these can only be thoroughly maintained where they spring out of a true religious faith and are quickened by the sense of duty done under yet higher and more ineffable sanctions than they can themselves supply. He was the son of poor but honest parents, who, falling into a strait, had emigrated to Van Dieman's Land. Young Walter worked hard and industriously. Many fine traits manifested themselves. The first payment he received from his employer he devoted to purchasing for his mother a sack of flour and a chest of tea. His sympathy was not confined to his own relationship. A poor man lamenting to him the straitness of his means and the largeness of his family, Walter suggested the possibility of improving his circumstances by starting as a dealer. The man replied hopelessly that the start required ten pounds—a sum which, in his state of hand to mouth dependence, he had no thought of ever possessing. Walter, seeing that his well meant advice had only served to make the poor fellow more painfully sensible of his utter helplessness, immediately gave him the ten pounds, although his own salary was but one hundred pounds a year. Mr. Powell subsequently went to Australia, where he prospered marvelously, and in a few years was very wealthy. One instance of his generosity, which gives a glimpse of his nobility of character, must not be omitted. Learning that Mr. Hargreave, the discoverer of the Australian gold-fields, was very little advantaged by a scientific revelation which had enriched so many thousands, Mr. Powell sent him anonymously £250, as an acknowledgement of his own personal indebtedness and his sense of Mr. Hargreave's claim to the public gratitude. He was at once active in business and faithful to conscience and God; full of energy, shrewd and deliberate, yet possessed of warm thoughts and impulses; quick to discern the signs of the times, yet never slow to do a brotherly service; keenly watchful to defeat all chicanery and over-reaching, yet never wearied in good works; calculating, yet trustful and tender, and more ambitious to benefit others than to hoard up for a problematic and distant future. And surely he was in all this the very ideal of the Christian merchant. Such a man truly ennobles trade.

REMARKABLE PRESENCE OF MIND.

> " Full fathom five thy father lies:
> Of his bones are coral made,"

sung Ariel to Ferdinand. Man never escaped that fate by a narrower chance than did Captain Hughes. Says a San Francisco paper:

On the last trip of the schooner Lola from Vallejo to this port, the wind having fallen off, and the vessel being in four fathoms of water, the anchor was let go, pursuant to the order of the master, Hughes, who had gone forward to give it. As the anchor was let slip, a two-and-a-half-inch line by which a buoy was made fast to its chain accidentally took a turn around the master's leg, and whipped him over the side and down into the sea. As he went rushing feet first to the bottom, he drew and opened a pocket knife, and with one desperate effort of strength against the pressure of the water he stooped downward and severed the line, having to cut deeply into the flesh of his leg to do so. As he shot up almost as swiftly as he had gone down, he returned his knife to his pocket, and when he reached the surface was picked up with only a lanced ankle as the result of what would have been a dive to death but for his coolness and nerve.

HEROIC CONDUCT AT MONMOUTH.

Most fitting and appropriate are the lines of the poet, Gallagher, when applied to the subject of this anecdote:

> Proud were they by such to stand,
> * * * * *
> To watch a battling husband's place,
> And fill it should he fall.

During the memorable battle of Monmouth—one long to be remembered in

Revolutionary annals—a gunner named Pitcher was killed. At the time he fell, his wife, who had followed him to the camp, and thence to the field of conflict, was bringing water to her husband from a spring. A call for some one to take the place of the fallen gunner was made. Instantly dropping the pail, the wife, Mary Pitcher—a "red-haired, freckeled-faced Irish woman," who was already distinguished for having fired the last gun at Fort Clinton, unhesitatingly stepped forward and offerd her services. She hastened to the cannon and seized the rammer, and with great skill and courage performed her husband's duty. The soldiers gave her the nick-name of "Captain Molly." On the day after the

MOLLIE PITCHER AT THE BATTLE OF MONMOUTH.

battle she was presented to General Washington, whose attention had been drawn to her act. He expressed his admiration of her bearing and her fidelity to her country, by conferring on her a sergeant's commission with half pay through life. Her bravery made her a great favorite among the French officers, and she would sometimes pass along the lines holding out her cocked hat, which they would nearly fill with crown pieces. Artemisia was scarcely more serviceable to Xerxes in the battle of Salamis, than Captain Molly to Washington in the battle of Monmouth. One served in a great Grecian expedition, to gratify her spirit, vigor of mind, and love of glory; the other fought, partly, it may be, to revenge the death of her husband, but more, doubtless, for the love she bore for an injured country, "bleeding at every vein." One was rewarded by a complete suit of Grecian armor; the other with a sergeant's commission, and both for their bravery. If the Queen of Caria is deserving of praise for her martial valor, the name of the heroic wife of the gunner should be woven with hers in a fadeless wreath of song.

DAUNTLESS JOHN JORDAN.

Among the first struggles of the late war was the Big Sandy campaign in Kentucky. The problem which the Union officers had to solve was, how to unite two wings of the army separated by an unknown country infested with roving bands of rebels and populated by disloyal people. This junction was to be formed in the face of a superior enemy, who would doubtless be apprised of every movement, and be likely to fall upon the separate columns the moment either was set in motion, in the hope of crushing them in detail. Evidently, the first thing to be done was to find a trustworthy messenger to convey dispatches between the two halves of the army. Colonel Moore, of the Fourteenth Kentucky, was applied to. "Have you a man," asked the commanding officer, "who will die rather than fail and betray us?" The Kentuckian reflected a moment, then answered: "I think I have; John Jordan, from the head of the Blaine." Jordan was sent for, and soon entered the tent of the Union commander. To the colonel he seemed a strange combination of cunning simplicity, undaunted courage and undoubting faith, but possessed of a quaint sort of wisdom, which ought to have given him to history. He was sounded thoroughly, for the fate of the campaign might depend upon his fidelity; but Jordan's soul was as clear as crystal. "Why did you come into this war?" at last asked the commander. "To do my part for the country, colonel," answered Jordan; "and I made no terms with the Lord. I gave him my life without conditions, and if he sees fit to take it in this tramp, why, it is his—I have nothing to say against it." "You mean you have come into the war not expecting to get out of it?" "I do, colonel." "Will you die rather than let this dispatch be taken?" "I will." The dispatch was written on tissue paper, rolled into the form of a bullet, coated with warm lead, and put into the hands of Jordan. He was given a carbine and a brace of revolvers, and mounting his horse when the moon was down he started on his perilous journey. The incidents of that perilous ride, in a hostile and unknown country, were interesting. Suffice it to say that Jordan delivered his message in safety, and the after history of the campaign is told when it is said that the Union wings did unite, and drove Humphrey Marshall from the state, thus preventing it from going out of the Union at that time. Subsequent exploits of Jordan proved him to be as heroic and determined as the present incident would indicate.

AN UNSELFISH ACT.

Several years ago a vessel left the harbor at San Francisco for a long voyage. Soon after leaving the port the clouds began to gather, the winds increased, and all hands were commanded to their posts in case of danger. The storm grew more formidable, and the vessel was turned again to the shore for safety. Upon nearing the shore an unseen rock stranded the vessel, and she commenced rapidly to fill. To save the vessel was now a hopeless thing, and everybody was ordered to take to the life-boat and save themselves. The moment was a trying one. Between life and death, with the wild billows of the deep lashing the sinking ship, and the heartless elements all combined to give the scene something of peculiar terror. The boats had left for the shore, bearing their precious burdens, but some were still on the vessel. A stout, dauntless man still stood on the deck. He was engaged in fastening several heavy belts of gold to his waist preparatory to plunging into the deep and swimming to the shore. Just as he was about to leap overboard he saw gazing piteously at him a little helpless girl, who begged him to save her life. Without a moment's hesitation, for the situation was becoming more trying every moment, he bravely unbuckled the precious belts from his body, rushed for the child and bade her cling tightly to his back. Rushing once more to the edge of the vessel he plunged overboard into the raging deep, sank, and rose again. It was a hard struggle, but he heroically battled against the overwhelming odds, and was finally dashed on a rock, severely injured. Ready and faithful hands were present and rescued the child, who escaped unhurt. They picked up the helpless hero and bore him to a place where attention could be given his wounds. It was found that he had sustained very serious injuries, such as would prostrate him for months. He was accordingly taken to a hospital, whither the little girl followed him; and during all those months of anguish and pain, when he was delirious and helpless, that little girl remained ever by his side; and when returning strength first began to manifest itse f, and he once more opened his eyes, the first thing he saw was his faithful nurse, the little girl whom he had so heroically rescued. The hero's name is not known, but his memory will not soon be forgotten, and when he comes to his final reward that act will form one of the brightest stars in his crown.

"OH, WHAT WILL MOTHER DO?"

These were the words of one of the bravest lads that shouldered a musket during the Rebel.ion. His name was Charles Carlton, and his home was at Franklin, Ohio. His words, repeated in the state senate, aroused Ohio to at once make provision for the widows and mothers of its soldiers. The incident occasioning the remark was one of the many during the Kentucky campaign. Garfield, with his college boys, is repelling an attack of an overwhelming number of confederates. For a moment there are signs of wavering, then their leader cal's out: "Every man to a tree! Give them as good as they send, my brave Bereans!" Though they are outnumbered ten to one they are able to hold their ground remarkably well. But soon the rebels, exasperated with the obstinate resistance, rush from cover and charge upon the little handful with the bayonet. Slowly they are driven down the hill, and two of them fall to the ground wounded. One never rises; the other, a lad of only eighteen, is shot through the thigh, and one of his comrades turns back to bear him to a place of safety. The advancing foe are within thirty feet, when one of them fires, and his bullet strikes a tree directly above the head of the Union soldier. He turns, levels his musket, and the foeman is in eternity. Then the rest are upon him; but, zigzagging from tree to tree, he is soon with his driven column. But not far are the brave boys driven. A few rods lower down they hear the voice of their leader: "To the trees again, my boys;" he cries "we may as well die here as in Ohio!"

To the trees they go, and in a moment the advancing horde is checked and then rolled backward. Up the hill they turn, firing as they go, and the little band follows. Soon the confederates reach the spot where the Berean boy lies wounded, and one of them says to him: " Boy, guv me yer musket." "Not the gun but its contents," returns the lad, and the rebel falls mortally wounded. Another raises his weapon to brain the prostrate lad, but he, too, falls, killed with his comrade's own rifle, and all this is done while the hero-lad is on the ground bleeding. An hour afterward his comrades bear him to a sheltered spot on the other side of the streamlet, and then the first word of complaint escapes him. As they are taking off his leg, he says, in his agony: "Oh, what will mother do?" There can be but little surprise felt that the Union cause was victorious, when such instances of bravery and devotion were so common among the soldiers.

WOMAN'S FIRMNESS.

In a New York village there resided a widow named Smith, who had sent four sons to the rebellion—two of whom were minors—leaving behind them only two sisters. After a while two of them returned home. Nathaniel Smith, a member of the Eighteenth Regiment, and the other a member of the Seventh Artillery, the latter on a furlough. One night there was to have been a jubilee at the house of their uncle, given in honor of the boys' return, and they had set off to meet companions, when, unexpectedly, officer Burt stepped up to Nathaniel and arrested him as a deserter. This was so unlooked for that he almost fainted on the spot. It appears that Nathaniel had deserted the regiment just previous to the second Bull Run battle, and since that time had been loitering about Washington and Alexandria, wholly unknown to the authorities in those places. He had enlisted at the breaking out of the Rebellion, and had he remained with his regiment he would have been mustered out of service in May. But he deserted eight months before his time was out, and consequently was compelled to make good that loss. After a parley with the officer who arrested him the latter consented to go with him back to his mother's house; and here a scene ensued which shows the earnest patriotism of a true woman's heart. Upon being informed of the circumstances she burst into a flood of tears and said: "I have sacrificed four sons to my country—two minors. I have buried my husband and children; but I have never known what trouble and grief were before. To have one brought back as a deserter is more than I can stand. I do not blame the officers for doing their duty, but I do you for deserting. Go, my son, you are bone of my bone, flesh of my flesh. I would rather have seen you brought home a corpse, than to find you alive, branded as a deserter. But go, my son; do your duty as a man and a soldier, remember that your mother's prayers are with you, and do not come home again until you can come as a man who has nothing to fear." While his mother was still engaged in talking to him in strains of sorrow and regret, his aunt came in—feeble in health, but strong in feeling. Mortified that he had deserted his comrades, she appealed to him as a lover of his country and a member of the family, to go back to the army and do his whole duty as a soldier and not return again until he had served his time out. The mother's and aunt's tears were too much for the soldier, for they both wept tears of regret. With their blessings, the soldier left them, promising henceforth to be a man, a true soldier, and not to return home until discharged.

YOUNG KNIGHTLY HEROES.

Two incidents of the praiseworthy deeds of boys form the basis of this sketch. One of the boys lives at Bay City, Michigan, and is named Kinderman. He has lost his right arm, but he did heroic work with his left. He and a younger brother were once fishing on Lake Michigan in a small boat, which a passing propeller upset. Young Kinderman seeing that his brother was likely to drown, seized him by the hair with his teeth and struck out for the shore. He swam with his left arm, until a boat which had put out from the shore picked him up.

The other young knight lives in Springfield, Mass., and at the time of the occurrence attended the high school of that city. While walking along the street he saw a dog making for a five-years-old boy, who was playing, not thinking of danger. The dog, apparently, was mad, for it held its head low and frothed at the mouth. Stepping at once in front of the child, the young hero, as soon as the dog came up, kicked it over. Then throttling it with one hand, he pounded its head with a stick until he killed it. In the terrible struggle the dog so bit him on the wrist as to leave three tooth-marks. These, when the dog was dead, he cauterized by coolly holding them over the flame of lighted matches. The child was uninjured. Some fifty years ago all England rang with the praises of Thomas Rowell Buxton—afterward Sir Thomas—for catching a mad dog, which was making toward a group of ladies, and holding it until chained. Buxton, however, was a stalwart Englishman with the strength of a Hercules. The Springfield hero was but a boy, who staked his life for a child.

GOULD, THE HERO OF CORINTH.

In the heat of the conflict, the Ninth Texas Regiment bore down upon the left center of the Twenty-Seventh Ohio Regiment with their battle flag at the head of the column, when Orrin B. Gould, a private of Company G, shot down the color-bearer and rushed forward for the confederate flag. A confederate officer shouted to his men to "*save the colors!*" and, at the same moment, put a bullet into the breast of Gould. But the young hero was not to be intimidated, with his flag-staff in his hand and the bullet in his breast he returned to his regiment, waving the former defiantly in the faces of the enemy. After the battle, on visiting the hospitals, Colonel Fuller, of the Twenty-Seventh Ohio, commanding the first brigade, second division, found young Gould stretched upon a cot, apparently in great pain. Upon seeing him, his face became radiant, and, pointing to his wound he said, "Colonel, I don't care for this, since I got their flag."

PAUL REVERE.

Can any one ever estimate the length and breadth of the bravery of the Revolutionary patriots? More sacred then than life itself was their country to them; and the haughty attitude of the mother country toward the feeble colonies only the firmer knit together their hopes and fears and their spirit of honest antagonism. In such a spirit was it that the daring deeds of men like Paul Revere were brought into existence. The midnight ride and the sounding of the alarm by this brave hero have long been lauded in poetry and song. Lexington is memorable as the scene of the first armed encounter in the Revolutionary contest. On the night of April 18, 1775, Paul Revere, of Boston, eluding the British sentinels, escaped into the country across Charles river and spread information of the intended march of a detachment of British troops to seize the provincial stores and the common at Concord. Lieutenant-Colonel Smith and Major Pitcairn, with a body of eight hundred British regulars, had, unnoticed, left Boston, and

PAUL REVERE'S MIDNIGHT RIDE.

soon were on the road to Concord. The moon shone brightly from the clear sky, and they moved on rapidly. To defeat the objects of this secret march of the British, Paul Revere rode as never a hero rode before. By preconcerted arrangement the light beaming from the tower of the old North church was to tell the moment their march began. From this quarter at last streamed a beacon light, while our hero was already far ahead announcing their coming. There was—

> " A hurry of hoofs in a village street,
> A shape in the moonlight, a bulk in the dark,
> And beneath from the pebbles, in passing, a spark
> Struck out by a steed flying fearless and fleet."

Soon the distant ringing of bells and firing of guns told the troops that the alarm was spreading. When they reached Lexington at dawn they found a small company of minute-men gathering on the village green. Riding up, Pitcairn shouted: "Disperse, you rebels! Lay down your arms!" "Too few to resist, too brave to fly," they hesitated. Discharging his pistol he cried aloud to his troops, "Fire!" The fate of the nation was with the dauntless Revere. The alarm spread fast, and the limited means of defense were brought into play. The first onset of the regulars was disastrous to the American cause, but bravery and determination such as these men possessed will not, cannot, be overcome. The result of Paul Revere's brave act cannot be measured. His was of that unselfish devotion to principle and country which is always honorable.

THE HEROINE OF MATAGORDA.

Did history not make mention of the achievement of our present heroine, it would not only do her injustice but the cause also in which she was interested.

In one of the old British battles the tempest had lasted for thirty hours, and sixty-four men out of one hundred and forty had fallen. The fort was not more than one hundred yards square; and "Here," says Napier, "be recorded an action of which it is difficult to say whether it was most feminine or heroic." The action referred to, as detailed in "The Eventful Life of a Soldier," won the woman for long after the sobriquet of "The Heroine of Matagorda." She was the wife of Sergeant Reston, of the Scots brigade. Under fire she tore up her linen to furnish bandages for the wounded; and water being wanted, a drummer boy was ordered to draw some from a well, but the scared child did not seem much inclined to the task, and lingered at the door of the hut with the bucket in his hand. "Why don't you go for the water?" asked the surgeon, angrily. "The puir bairn is frightened," said Mrs. Reston, "and no wonder; gie the bucket to me." And under all that storm she proceeded coolly to the well, procuring water for the wounded. General Napier states that a shot cut the bucket-rope in her hand, but she recovered it, and fulfilled her mission. "Her attention to the wounded was beyond all praise," says Sergeant Donaldson, of the 94th; "she carried sand-bags for the repair of the batteries, and handed ammunition, wine and water to the men at the guns. I think I see her yet," he adds, "while the shot and shell were flying thick around her, bending her body to shield her child from danger by the exposure of her own person." She died at an old age in Glasgow, without other token to her merit than that accorded by the humble book of her husband's comrade.

ALL A MOTHER CAN DO.

At the time of the first call for volunteers to strike down the Rebellion, a matronly lady, accompanied by her son, a fine youth of about nineteen years, entered a gun store on Broadway, New York, and purchased a full outfit for him; selecting the best weapons and other articles for a soldier's use, that could be found in the store, she paid the bill, remarking, with evident emotion, "This, my son, is all that I can do, I have given you up to serve your country, and may

God go with you. It is all that a mother can do." The scene attracted considerable attention, and tearful eyes followed that patriotic mother and her son as they departed from the place.

INTREPIDITY OF MRS. ISRAEL.

During the Revolution Israel Israel, a true Whig and a worthy farmer, residing on the banks of the Delaware, near Wilmington, was, for a short time, a prisoner on board the frigate Roebuck, directly opposite his own house and land. While thus situated, it was reported by some loyalists by whose treachery he had been betrayed into the hands of the enemy, that he had said repeatedly that "He would sooner drive his cattle as a present to George Washington than to receive thousands of dollars in British gold for them." The commander hearing the report, to be revenged on the rebel sent a small detachment of soldiers to drive his cattle, which were in plain sight of the frigate, down to the Delaware, and have them slaughtered before their owner's eyes. Mrs. Israel, who was young and sprightly, and brave as a Spartan, seeing the movements of the soldiers as she stood in her doorway, and divining their purpose as they marched toward the meadow where the cattle were grazing, called a boy about eight years old, and started off in great haste to defeat, if possible, their marauding project. They threatened and she defied, till at last they fired at her. The cattle, more terrified than she, scattered over the fields; and as the balls flew thicker she called on the little boy "Joe" the louder and more earnestly to help, determined that the assailants should not have one of the cattle. They did not. She drove them all into the barn-yard, when the soldiers, out of respect to her courage, or for some other cause, ceased their molestations and returned to the frigate.

AN OBSCURE PATRIOT.

Strategy oftentimes manifests a spirit of more bravery and undaunted courage than is generally conceded. During the Rebellion much was accomplished on both sides by this forcible agent. One of the most striking illustrations of this fact is related of a noble boy. The fact that General Buckner did not take the city of Louisville instead of stopping at Green River, where he invaded Kentucky on the line of the Louisville and Nashville Railroad, was due, not to any foresight or force of the United States authorities or of the Union men of Kentucky, but to the loyalty, courage and tact of one obscure individual. The secessionists had laid their plans to appear suddenly in Louisville with a powerful force. They had provided for transportation four hundred cars and fifteen locomotives, and had eight thousand men, with artillery and camp equipage, on board. They had secured the services of the telegraph operators, one of whom forwarded to Louisville a dispatch explaining the detention of the trains on the road, and things were moving along in good order. Louisville, with perhaps a few exceptions on the part of some secessionists, was unsuspecting and unguarded—General Anderson being innocent of any knowledge of the movement. But at a station just beyond Green River there was a young man in the service of the road who was a warm friend of the Union cause, and who, comprehending the meaning of the monster train when it came up, seized a crowbar used for taking up rails to make repairs, and while the locomotives were being wooded and watered, ran across a curve, and in a deep, narrow cut wrenched the spikes from four rails. The train came along at good speed; the rails spread, the locomotive plunged into the ground, the cars crashed on the top of it, and it was twenty-four hours before the train could go ahead. In the meantime Louisville was saved. The hero of the occasion had not had time to get out of the cut before the crash came, and was taken, but in the general confusion got away and was safe. That obscure individual did much more for his country than some who wore stars and straps.

NOTHING LOST BY TRUE COURAGE.

An illustration of the spirit of the brave men who fought the battle of good government against treason will be found in the following—though this is but one of a thousand similar noble and heroic instances:

A New Hampshire regiment had been engaged in several successive battles, very bloody and very desperate, and in each engagement had been distinguishing themselves more and more; but their successes had been very dearly bought, both in men and officers. Just before the taps the word came that the fort they had been investing was to be stormed by daybreak the next morning, and they were invited to lead the "forlorn hope." For a time the brain of the colonel fairly reeled with anxiety. The post of honor was the post of danger, but in view of all circumstances would it be right, by the acceptance of such a proposition, to involve his already decimated regiment in utter annihilation? He called his long and well-tried chaplain into council with him, and, asking what was best to be done, the chaplain advised him to let the men decide for themselves. At the colonel's request he stated to the regiment all the circumstances. Not one in twenty, probably, would be left alive after the first charge; scarcely one of the entire number would escape death, except as they would be wounded or taken prisoners. Having submitted the matter to the soldiers the chaplain told them to "Think it over calmly and deliberately, and come back at twelve o'clock and let us know your answer." True to the appointed time they all returned. "All?" was the interrogatory. "Yes, sir, all, without exception, and all of them ready for service or for sacrifice." "Now," said the chaplain, "go to your tents and write your letters; settle all your wordly business, and whatever sins you have upon your consciences unconfessed or unforgiven, ask God to forgive them. As usual, I will go with you, and the Lord do with us as seemeth him good." The hour came, the assault was made; onward those noble spirits rushed into "the imminent deadly breach," right into the jaws of death. But, like Daniel when he was thrown into the lions' den, it pleased God that the lions' mouths should be shut. Scarcely one hour before the enemy had secretly evacuated the fort, and the "forlorn hope" entered into full possession, without the loss of a single man.

RIGHT ARM STILL LEFT

Our country can never fully repay the courageous sacrifices made by the gallant boys in blue during the late war drama. The wounds, the haggard expressions, and the broken constitutions tell a tale of horror and bloodshed, all for the love, of country. Is there any reason, then, why the government, made secure by their sufferings, should not amply repay them so far as it is possible? Judge Kelly once entered the office of Mr. Stanton, Secretary of War, having with him a youthful looking officer whose empty coat-sleeve hung from his left shoulder. He was introduced to the secretary as Brevet Lieutenant Harry Rockafellow, of Philadelphia. "My friend," said the judge, "left a situation worth eight hundred dollars a year, three days after the president's proclamation for troops, to carry a musket at eleven dollars a month, with his regiment, the New York seventy-first. After the term of his enlistment had expired, he marched with his regiment to Bull Run. Early in the day he received that ugly rifle ball in his mouth"—pointing to a minnie ball that hung to his watch key—"and for two hours and a half he carried it in his fractured jaw-bone, fighting like a true hero until a cannon ball took off his arm and rendered him powerless. He was captured, and for three long months lay in a mangled condition in a tobacco warehouse in Richmond without proper surgical treatment. He was breveted a lieutenant by his colonel for his bravery, and is now filling a small clerkship. I beg of you to appoint him in the regular service." "But where could I put him if I were to?" said Mr. Stanton. The judge was about to reply, when the young man raised his arm and said, with an anxious look: "See, I have a right arm still, and General Kearney has only his left. Send me into the line, where there is fighting to be done! I have letters from——" He tried to draw a bundle of letters from his pocket. Mr. Stanton stopped him. "Put up your letters, sir; you have spoken for yourself. Your wish shall be granted. The country cannot afford to neglect such men as you!" Ere the soldier could thank him for his kindness, the case was noted. He turned to leave, and remarked to the judge: "I shall be proud of my commission, for I feel that I have earned it. This day is the proudest one of my whole life!" His head seemed so light that he appeared not to realize the loss he had met with, nor the weary nights and long, long days he had suffered in the vile prisons of the enemy. Such sentiments and such incidents are but the results of patriotism and bravery, which the boys in blue so largely possessed.

A WOUNDED HERO.

A very remarkable and praise-worthy incident is related of a young man, a soldier of the thirty-first regiment of Illinois volunteers, when in the battles of the Rebellion. In one of the conflicts he received a musket-shot wound in the right thigh, the ball passing through the intervening flesh and lodging in the left thigh. The boy repaired to the rear and applied to the surgeon to dress his wound. He, however, was observed to manifest a peculiar reserve in the matter, requesting the doctor to keep his misfortune a secret from his comrades and officers. He then asked the surgeon if he would dress his wound at once, in order that he might be enabled to return to the fight. The physician told him that he was in no condition to return, and that he had better go to the hospital; but the young brave insisted upon going back, offering as an argument in favor of it the fact that he had fired twenty-two rounds after receiving his wound, and he was confident he could fire as many more after his wound should be dressed. The surgeon found he could not prevent his returning to the field, so he attended to his wants, and the young soldier went off to rejoin his comrades in their struggles, and remained dealing out his ammunition to good account until the day was over, as if nothing had happened him. Several days after he returned to the doctor to have his wound re-dressed, and continued to pay him daily visits in his leisure hours, attending to duty in the meantime.

TENDER BURIAL OF A UNION DRUMMER BOY BY TWO GIRLS.

The following incident is as touching as it is tender and heroic:

After the battle of Bean Station, the confederate soldiers gave loose play to all manner of indignities toward the slain. They stripped their bodies, and shot persons who came near the battlefield to show any attention to the dead. The body of a little drummer boy was left naked and exposed. Near by, in an humble house, there were two young girls, the eldest but sixteen, who resolved to give the body a decent burial. They took the night for their task. With a hammer and nails in hand, and boards on their shoulders, they sought the place where the body of the dead drummer boy lay. From their own scanty ward obe they clothed the body for the grave. With their own hands they made a rude coffin in which they tenderly put the dead body. They dug the grave and lowered the body into it, and covered it over. The noise of the hammering brought some of the rebels to the spot; the sight was too much for them. Not a word was spoken, no one interfered; and when the sacred rites of the burial were performed all departed, and the little drummer boy lay in undisturbed rest in the grave dug by gentle maiden's hands on the battle field. Such tenderness and devotion deserves to run along the line of coming generations with the story of the woman who broke the alabaster box on the loved head of the Savior, and with her who of her penury cast her two mites into the treasury.

SENTIMENTS OF A DYING SOLDIER.

At a public meeting in Boston, Mr. Gough once said: "Not long since I was in a hospital, and saw a young man, twenty-six years of age, pale and emaciated, with his shattered arm resting upon an oil-silk pillow; and there he had been for many long weary weeks, waiting for sufficient strength for an amputation. I knelt by his side and said: 'Will you answer me one question?' 'Yes, sir,' was his reply. 'Suppose you were well, at home, in good health, and knew all this would come to you if you enlisted, would you enlist?' 'Yes, sir,' he answered in a whisper, 'I would in a minute! What is my arm or my life, compared with the safety of the country?' That was patriotism of the genuine brand."

A TYPICAL AMERICAN HERO—JAMES A. GARFIELD.

The life and character of all others which the American people delight to honor and which the whole civilized world admires for its bravery, nobility, and heroic devotion to duty, is that of James A. Garfield. The incidents of his life are numerous and interesting, but in none is a spirit other than integrity and honesty of purpose manifested. The life of Garfield is the one which to-day is molding the character of the rising generation, and its influence will be felt as long as Americans love to honor the deeds of a hero. There is nothing of affectation in professing love for the martyred president. The awful trial that came so suddenly after his new honors, he bore without a murmur. In that unparalleled affliction all classes of the people were drawn to him, watched by his bedside, prayed for him day and night through the melancholy hours of his illness, and felt as if he belonged to them. Through all his life, as a boy and man, as a soldier, as a statesman and a president, but one controlling purpose runs.

The early years of our hero's life were passed in uncomfortable poverty. But referring to this in after life, he gives us the key-note of his life and the motives which spurred him onward. In an address to the students of Hiram College he said: "Poverty is uncomfortable, as I can testify, but nine cases out of ten the best thing that can happen to a young man is to be tossed overboard and compelled to sink or swim for himself. In all my acquaintance I never knew a man to be drowned who was worth the saving." Deprived of a father's care when of very tender age, he was early compelled to do for himself, and almost the first words that his lips made audible pledged attention and care for his mother. When James was twelve years of age the family were still in indigent circumstances. The embryo president has obtained a few tools with which he shows great dexterity. He mends the chairs, puts latches and hinges on the doors, and is so handy that his brother Thomas says he will "surely be a carpenter some day and build houses." During the winters the children were permitted to attend school for a short time, and now our hero's eagerness for books begins to manifest itself. Fired by reading the exciting recitals of Napoleon's victories, he once exclaimed enthusiastically: "Mother, when I get to be a man I am going to be a soldier."

Every reader is acquainted largely with our subject's early life. Of his experience as canal hand, his early conversion, life at Hiram, and college experience at Williams, the many recitals have made them seemingly trite and common. When Lincoln's famous manifesto went forth to the country, Garfield was in the Ohio Senate. At the call being read in the Senate for seventy-five thousand men, Senator Garfield was instantly on his feet, and amid the tumultuous acclamations from the assemblage, moved that twenty thousand troops and three millions of money should be at once voted as Ohio's quota! His speech was immediately illustrated by offering his own services in any capacity Governor Dennison might choose. That he should uphold the flag was demanded both by patriotism and by the logic of the republican doctrine that he had so nobly, so bravely upheld. It was but the second stage of resistance to slavery. While waiting a wider field he occupied himself with the arming of the militia or any measure that had for its object the advancement of the plans then in progress. Subsequently he was offered the lieutenant-colonelcy of the forty-second Ohio regiment, but did not accept the proffered command hastily. Not caring to grasp the glitter of command with the avidity of an aspirant for honors, he went home, opened his mother's Bible and pondered upon the subject. He had a wife, a child, and a few thousand dollars. If he gave his life to the country, would God and the few thousand dollars provide for his wife and child? Finally deciding in the affirmative, he wrote a friend as follows: "I regard my life as given to the country. I am only anxious to make as much of it as possible before the mortgage on it is foreclosed." In the field as elsewhere Garfield was ever true to himself, and his brilliant actions especially in the Kentucky campaign and in the battle of Chickamauga will never be forgotten. While in the South Garfield received a letter informing him of his nomination to congress from the Ashtabula district, which upon consultation with his co-officers he decided to accept. Rosecrans, in advising him upon the subject, said: "Be true to yourself, and you will make your mark before the country." How much of truth that sentiment contained the great general himself did not then imagine. After a week or two further service, he was sent as bearer of dispatches to Washington. He there learned of his promotion to a major-generalship of vol-

unteers "for gallant and meritorious conduct at the battle of Chickamauga."
The certainty of assignment to important commands seemed to augur a brilliant
future. No man had a keener sense of justice than General Garfield. One day
a fugitive slave came rushing into the camp with a bloody head and apparently
frightened almost to death. He had only passed my tent, says a staff officer of
General Sherman, when in a moment a regular bully of a fellow came riding up
and with a volley of oaths began to ask after his "nigger." General Garfield
was not present, and he passed on to the division commander, who happened to
be a sympathizer with the theory that fugitives should be returned to their mas-
ters, and that the Union soldiers should be made instruments for returning them.
He accordingly wrote a mandatory order to General Garfield, in whose command
the darkey was supposed to be hiding, telling him to hunt up and deliver over
the property of the outraged citizen. The staff officer who brought the order
stated the case fully to General Garfield before handing him the order, well
knowing the general's strong anti-slavery views. The general took the order,
and after reading it carefully, deliberately wrote on it the following indorsement: "I respectfully but positively decline to allow my command to search for
or deliver up any fugitive slaves. I conceive that they are here for quite another purpose. The command is open and no obstacles will be placed in the
way of the search." When the staff officer read the general's indorsement, he
was inclined to be frightened and remonstrated with Garfield's determination.
He said if he returned the order in that shape to the division commander he
certainly would arrest and court-martial the writer. To this the Ohio general
replied: "The matter may as well be tested first as last. Right is right, and I do
not propose to mince matters at all. My soldiers are here for far other purposes
than hunting and returning fugitive slaves." As was natural, the division commander was highly incensed, and sent for Garfield at once. The brave general
stoutly defended his position, and gave his superior such a lecture as to make
him think possibly he was in the wrong. No court-martial was ordered, and
thereafter the division commander refrained from issuing orders on the subject
of slavery. In the battle of Chickamauga Garfield was one of the principal
actors, and his bravery there will ever appear in brightest hues.

> " Undaunted 'mid the whirlwind storm of war,
>   The shock of surging foes, the wild dismay
>   Of shattered legions swept in blood away,
> While the red conflict, thundering afar,
>   Raged on the left—yet all unseen, unknown—
>   Great chieftain! man of men! 'twas thine alone,
> With faith and courage high, the guiding star
>   Of that disastrous field, to seek the fray
>   Where still the hosts of Union hold their own,
> With wasting lines that stand, and strive, and bleed,
>   Waiting the promise of a better day.
> O steadfast soul! O heart of oak! No harm
> Could reach thee then: thou hadst for shield His arm
> Who kept thee for the nation's later need."

So sudden was that famous rout made that the stream of fugitives, swarming
back from the woods, was the first information received by the Union officers

that the line had been pierced. There was no time to be lost. Behind the fleeing troops came the iron columns of the enemy. Hastily gathering his precious maps, Garfield followed Rosecrans, on horseback, over to the Dry Valley road. Here Garfield dismounted, and exerted all his power to stem the tide of retreat. Snatching a flag from a flying color-bearer he shouted at the deaf ears of the mob. Seizing men by the shoulders he would turn them around, and then grasp others to try and form a nucleus to resist the flood. It was useless. The moment he would take his hands off a man he would run. Rejoining Rosecrans, who believed that the entire army was routed, the commander said: "Garfield, what can be done?" Undismayed by the panic stricken army crowding past him, which is said to be the most demoralizing and unnerving sight on earth, Garfield calmly said, "One of us should go to Chattanooga, secure the bridge in case of total defeat, and collect the fragments of the army on a new line. The other should make his way, if possible, to Thomas, explain the situation, and tell him to hold his ground at any cost, until the army can be rallied at Chattanooga." "Which will you do?" asked Rosecrans. "Let me go to the front," was General Garfield's instant reply. "It is dangerous," said he, "but the army and country can better afford for me to be killed than for you." After a brief consultation, a painful suspense, a few more hurried words, then a grasp of the hands, and the commander and chief of staff separated, the one to go to the rear, the other to the front. Rosecrans has said that he felt Garfield would never come back again. Then began that world-famous ride. No one knew the situation of the troops, or the cause of the disaster, and the way to retrieve it, like the chief of staff. To convey that priceless information to Thomas, Garfield determined to do or die. It was a race between the rebel column and the noble steed on which Garfield rode. Up and down the stony valley road, sparks flying from the horses' heels, two of Garfield's comrades hatless, and all breathless, without delay or doubt, on dashed the heroes. Still the enemy was between them and Thomas. At last Garfield said, "We must try to cross now or never. In a half hour it will be too late for us to do any good." Turning sharply to their right, they found themselves in a dark, tangled forest. They were scratched and bleeding from the brier thickets and the overhanging branches. But not a rider checked his horse. General Garfield's horse seemed to catch the spirit of the race. Over ravines and fences, through an almost impenetrable undergrowth, sometimes through a marsh, and then over broken rocks, the smoking steed plunged without a quiver. Suddenly they came upon a cabin, a Confederate pest house. A crowd of unfortunates, in various stages of the small-pox were sitting and lying about the lonely and avoided place. The other riders spurred on their way, but General Garfield reined in sharply and, calling in a kind tone to the strongest of the wrecks, asked, "Can I do anything for you, my poor fellow?" In an instant the man gasped out, "Do not come near. It is small-pox. But for God's sake give us money to buy food." Quick as thought the great-hearted chief of staff drew out his purse and tossed it to the man, and with a rapid but cheerful "goodby," spurred after his companions. Crashing, tearing, plunging, rearing, through the forest dashed the steed. Poet's song could not be long in celebrating that daring deed. All the while General Garfield was in the most imminent danger. But of personal danger he never thought. The great fear in his mind was that he would fail to reach Thomas. At last they reached a cotton-field. If the enemy was near it was almost certain death. Suddenly a rifle-ball whizzed past Garfield's face. Turning in his saddle he saw the fence on the right glittering with murderous rifles. A second later a shower of bullets rattled around the little party. Garfield shouted, "Scatter, gentlemen, scatter," and wheeled abruptly to the left. The two orderlies with him fell, and Garfield became the single target for the enemy. His own horse received two balls, but the noble animal kept straight on at a terrific speed. General Garfield, speaking of it afterward, said that his thought was divided between poor Thomas, and his young wife and child in the little home at Hiram. With a few more leaps he gained a place of safety. Thomas was yet a mile away, but the brave Garfield was soon by his side, explaining the nature of the situation. W ile so doing his noble horse, which had borne him on his memorable ride, dropped dead. It was a terrible struggle; and the storm of battle raged with fearful power. But all the valor and all the fury of the Confederates was in vain. "George A. Thomas," in the words of Garfield, "was indeed the 'rock of Chickamauga,' against which the wild waves of battle dashed in vain. The field was saved to the Union army, and that act which more than all others contributed to the victory was the brave, clear-headed, dauntless, courageous ride of General Garfield. The spirit of bravery, which finds its highest expression in this exploit, was always a prominent part of Garfield's character.

Even when the great party of his choice had made him their standard bearer, and it was plain that the highest honors at the disposal of the nation were about to be showered upon him, he was still the same unpretentious, noble man. As the time for the election approached, it became more and more apparent to his friends that the mere question of his personal success or failure was insignificant to him as a factor in the contest. He wished for success infinitely more for the sake of the gratification it would give to his friends than for any power, emolument or honor that should come to him. Bidding a near friend good- y only a few days before the election, he said, with a touch of almost boyish humor, "You will not think any the less of me if I am not elected, will you?" Soon after the election General Garfield announced his purpose to be "a first-class listener," and patiently and philosophically received the advice and suggestions of his party friends concerning the shaping of his course. Through all the enthusiasm and ceremonial of the inauguration there was still the same calm, intellectual poise, the same perfect self-control and mastery. The glories of the present were brilliant and attractive enough, but to him the future brought a sobering, saddening prospect. "Four years hence," said he, "I shall leave the presidency, still a young man, but with no future before me, to become a political reminiscence—a squeezed lemon, to be thrown away."

Probably no administration ever opened its existence under brighter auspices than that of President Garfield, but it was not long before his great vitality showed visible signs of yielding to the dragging wear of the never-ending demands and importunities for place. Each day brought its exhausting physical fatigue and intellectual weariness—the result of a continual din of selfish talk. Fairly staggering into the library at the close of a specially exhausting day, he once said: "I cannot endure this much longer; no man, who has passed his prime, can succeed me here, to wrestle with the people as I have done, without its killing him." The president was scarcely free from the anxiety of his mother's illness in the late spring, before she, whose light and comfort had done more to make his life happy than all his achievements and triumphs, was prostrated by a dangerous illness. Dividing his time between the cares of his office and her chamber, he gave her that devotion which was to be so soon, so amply and so heroically repaid. With the startling events of the fateful 2nd of July, and the incidents of the memorable eighty days, the reader is almost as familiar as if he had stood in the place of those whose privilege it was to minister to him. It has been remarked that the president scarcely referred to his assassin. He seems to have foreshadowed his feelings in one of his little speeches during the campaign, in which he said: "If a man murders you without provocation, your soul bears no burden of the wrong, but all the angels of the universe will weep for the misguided man who committed the murder." When Mrs. Garfield thinks of the seriousness with which he would send her away from him, when he would say, "Yes, go and ride; I want you to;" "You must go to bed now; I can't let you sit up any longer," or "Go down to the table; you must preside there," she wonders that she dared to leave him, even for a moment, yet his gentle firmness compelled obedience and went far to encourage the hope in which she lived. Even that first night, when he said to her, "Go, now, and rest; I shall want you near me when the crisis comes," she did not, or would not, think that he referred to his death, although she afterward knew he did. The tenderness with which he withheld from her what she now believes he felt would be his fate, deluges her heart with tears.

Thus Garfield lived. To moralize on the life and works of this grand American would be superfluous. He has furnished to the people of the United States one of the brightest and noblest examples of American citizenship. Both in public life and private life he has contributed to the annals of our times a record unsullied as the azure sky. His steps were the steps of a pure man climbing up to greatness. His ambitions were chastened, his aspirations the aspirations of a patriot. Over his great talents was shed the luster of noble activities, and his path was illumined with something of the effulgence of genius. His integrity was spotless, his virtue white as the snow. Of all our public men of recent times, Garfield was, in a certain sense, the most American. He had suffered all the hardships of the common lot. He had known poverty and orphanage and toil. To himself he owed, in a pre-eminent degree, his victory over adversity and his rise to distinction. He carried into public life, even to the highest seat of honor, the plainness and simplicity of a man of the people. Ostentation was no part of his nature, and subtlety found no place in his practices. In an age of venality and corruption—the very draff and ebb of the civil war—he stood unscathed. He went up to his high seat and down to the doorway of the grave without the scent of fire on his garments. His name smells sweet in all lands under the circle of the sun, and his fame is a priceless legacy which posterity will not willingly let die.